Remembering the Summer of the Pink Flamingoes

A Novel by
J. Scott Sawyer

PublishAmerica
Baltimore

Hardcover 978-1-4489-4553-5
Softcover 978-1-4489-7592-1
PUBLISHED BY PUBLISHAMERICA, LLLP
www.publishamerica.com
Baltimore

Printed in the United States of America

To Mignonne, Clay, and Cameron.

My love. My happiness. My life.

Nothing in my world would be possible without you guys.

I love you!

ACKNOWLEDGMENTS

As any writer knows, it takes more than one person to complete a book, and I would like to thank the many special people who have helped me.

Thanks to Publish America for taking a chance on me and for all of their guidance and patience. The people I have dealt with during this process have been extremely helpful and wonderful!

Thank you so much to all of my family and friends who have been so supportive and encouraging.

A very big thank you to Marybeth Colman, Stephanie Eastep, Melanie Edwards, Barbara Ellis, Lesa Hay, Sandi Inman, Janet Pruitt, Pam Redus, Anita Sawyer, Mignonne Sawyer, Gayla Simmons, and Missy Willoughby for reading my rough drafts and offering their wonderful advice, many corrections, and creative ideas to the story.

My heartfelt thanks to all of the English teachers who have been so influential in my life, especially Kathy Jones.

Thank you to David Dietzen for his push so long ago to put my words on paper.

Thank you to my Mom, Dad, Brother and Sister for their love and continually telling me this was possible.

Thanks to Melanie Edwards, Pat Frensley, Brian (Chuckwagon) Lane, and Jon Wilson for being the true characters of the story. I am so happy to have had, and still have, these wonderful friends in my life.

And finally, thank you with all of my heart to my wonderful wife, Mignonne, and my two incredible sons, Clay and Cameron, for their love, patience, and understanding while I spent so many hours on the computer.

ONE

BRRRIIINNG!

There are few things that cause your heart to beat faster than the phone ringing after midnight. Once your breathing has calmed a bit, and you've swallowed your heart back down into your chest, you find yourself praying that it's a wrong number or someone's fax machine calling your home number by mistake. But it was to be neither this night. It was the call everyone dreads.

"Hello."

"Scott?"

"Yes." I glance at the clock, 2:30 a.m., Tuesday.

"It's Pat."

"Hey, Pat." I rub my eyes and try to prepare myself for what's coming. It's two-thirty a.m. here in Hawaii so that means it's six-thirty a.m. in Tennessee. Pat and I have been friends since high school and we still talk regularly but he would never call this late if it weren't bad.

"I'm sorry to call so late, but I have bad news." Pat's voice is trembling like it's all he can do to keep it together. "Jason Maler...was killed last night."

My lungs deflate as if someone drove a knife through them and my settling heart makes another attempt to escape through my throat. Jason Maler was an original member of our gang.

"Oh my...," is all I can say even though a thousand thoughts are running through my mind. Pat Wilson and I first buddied up when we were ten years old. Jason moved into the house next to Pat's during spring break four years later. He was a year older than us but had been held back a year so he was in the same eighth grade class. Jason was a big country hick kid from Arkansas who always seemed utterly lost and hopeless. It was sad for this kid to be just fifteen and already socially doomed along with the drugstore cowboys who had never ridden a horse or with the hippie freaks who acted like they had experienced Vietnam.

Pat and had I steered clear of him most of that spring semester seeing as how we were sort of on the popular side and being seen with or, even worse, having a friend like Jason could seriously damage or possibly destroy our cool status. But once summer break began and we noticed the kid playing by himself in his yard and caught him following us into town a couple of times, we began to feel sorry for him and decided we would make him our project and help him fit in.

Pat let the news of Jason's death sink in for a moment, and then gave me the details.

"Sherry called me a little while ago. Apparently Jason still had her listed as who to contact in case of emergency."

"Jeez," slips from my mouth. Jason and Sherry Masters had been on and off together for over twenty years but never married.

My wife begins to stir and rolls over.

"Pat, hold on while I change phones." I push the hold button, grab my robe and go down the hall to my office. I take a deep breath and pick up the receiver. "Okay, I'm back."

Pat clears his voice and continues. "She said that the police found a car partially submerged in the river near her house. They went down the bank to investigate and found Jason slumped over the steering wheel. His face was covered in blood so they figure he lost control, went down the bank and slammed into a big rock. He wasn't wearing his seat belt. They think the impact against the windshield must have broken his neck or something."

Pat stops talking and I realize I need to say something.

"What about the airbag?"

Pat exhales a long sigh. "He was in the Camaro."

"The '72?" The sweetest car any of us ever had until he hit a tree and jammed the driver's door stuck while avoiding the dog of a girl he wanted to date. I got to drive the car a lot that summer because I was thin enough to crawl through the driver's window. "He still had that thing?"

"Yeah." Pat answers. "No airbags."

By the time we began ninth grade the three of us had achieved a sort of legendary status. It had been an incredible Summer, not just because we had turned Jason into an acceptable, fairly popular kid, but because of an incredible event involving flamingoes that occurred that August. Getting your picture in the local Franklin paper was a life altering event in itself, but having a feature story about you appear in the statewide paper, *The Tennessean*, was monumental.

The following summer, after tenth grade, Jason turned sixteen and had bought a '72 cream colored Camaro from a junk dealer and spent a year restoring it, finally finishing it right before our senior year. We had some of the best times of our young lives cruising in that car. And the girls, well, they *loved* the car but didn't necessarily love Jason. Even though Pat and I had worked on him becoming cool, deep down he was still that big hick kid and after a couple of dates *that* part of him came out and the girls sort of…ran. He wasn't a bad guy by any means just not the guy they were looking for. Even though he laughed about it, his heart broke a bit more each time.

"Scott," Pat asks. "Are you listening?"

"Sorry, Pat. What else?"

"That's all I know at this point. Except…"

"Except what?" I prompt.

"Sherry said the police found a note about a letter."

"What note? Where?"

"It was on him, in his jacket pocket."

I think the worst. "What did it say, Pat?" I ask. There is a brief silence. "Pat?"

"The note was to Sherry. It said she was to contact you about a letter Jason left for you in the event of his death."

"What did it say?"

"Don't know. It's with Jason's attorney, a woman named Lucinda Evans, so you're the only one who can open it."

I wonder what in the world he would have been writing to me.

"You want us to mail it to you?"

I think about it; I really do. I actually consider having him mail the letter. Have I really become that much of a jerk?

"No, Pat. I'll read it when I get there."

"Good," Pat says. "I'm glad you're coming."

There is a long silence between the two of us. I finally break it.

"Pat, had you talked to him recently?"

"Not for a while. We saw each other around, but he seemed…preoccupied," Pat says. "You?"

"No. It's probably been a year." More needs to be said but the words don't come. I know I will have many hours on the plane to sort out my thoughts. I glance over at the wall clock, three-thirty. "I'll call the airline in a couple of hours and see when I can catch a flight out."

"Okay," Pat says. "Just call me with your flight info and I'll let you know if I have any more details here.

"That'll work."

"All right. Talk with you later, Scott."

"Pat."

"Yeah?"

"Thanks for calling."

It's been five years since I crossed the country to visit my old hometown, Franklin, Tennessee. My life now flourishes across the Pacific in a state known as Paradise. I am a writer, novelist or author, however you want to phrase it. My career began with magazine features and newspaper articles, then a children's book that did fairly well, and finally a novel that went to number two on the best seller list. That was when I learned the valuable lesson to *not* release a novel at the same time John Grisham does. A year later, at the age of twenty-seven, my second novel went to number one and the movie rights to both books sold. In my mind I had made the big time and didn't need to stay in some small no name Southern town. I told my family and friends I was heading to the beach and hoped they would visit because I didn't see myself coming back any time soon. Funny really, that pact of our youth so many of us have made. Why is it that we think of ourselves as failures if we remain in our hometown?

I hang up the phone and sit for about fifteen minutes before the reality of what is happening sets in. The tears come quickly and soon the sobs. It surprises me, this sudden surge of emotion, regret, and loss over someone I haven't thought enough of to call or send a card to in years.

I hear a noise and glance up. My wife, Mignonne, or Mig, as I call her, stands in the doorway, tears in her own eyes, not for Jason; she didn't know about him yet. Her tears are for me. I tell her what has happened and she leads me to our balcony overlooking the North Shore. We lay in the hammock and she holds me until sunrise. She asks if I want her to come with me and I do, but both kids have school projects and she has a huge presentation at the University of Hawaii, so I tell her I can go by myself.

She is a professor of literature and has written a non-fiction book about the degradation of literature by commercial fiction, which is, of course, what I write. Her book climbed to number thirty-three on the non-fiction charts and sold fairly well. She *has* read my books, not out of interest, but purely out of love. She sweetly refers to them as entertaining and she does like the money they make.

TWO

I call Delta Airlines at six o'clock *a.m.*and speak to a very nice woman named Cindy. She has said they have a flight to Los Angeles at three p.m. and after a two hour layover I can catch a connection to Nashville. She's sorry about my friend but is happy to have me flying her airline.

I decide not to call Pat back with my flight information. It has been so many years since I've been home, I want to drive myself and have some time alone to drive through town.

My immediate family moved away from Franklin a few years ago. Mom and Dad retired and followed my brother, Tim, to Florida. He teaches underprivileged kids at an inner city school in Miami. Mom and Dad always said that if we were going to move away it had better be somewhere fun or else they wouldn't waste their vacation time visiting. I fly them to Hawaii once a year and also see them whenever book tours take me to the southeast.

The flight to California is quiet and uneventful which is great, especially considering I'm flying in coach. Even though I'm successful, I just can't *always* justify first class, unless of course my publisher is paying. The layover in Los Angeles is, as expected, longer than two hours. I don't know why airline companies can't just tell us the truth. *"We'll leave when we're ready to leave."* Lucky for me though, the coach seats from L.A. to Nashville are over-booked and because I am a frequent flyer, I'm getting bumped to first class straight through to Nashville.

After four hours, I finally board the plane and find my seat in the back row of the luxury section. My wife has packed her new manuscript, called, "Why Authors Sell Their Literary Talent to Fiction," in my carry on bag hoping I can give it a read through and offer any suggestions, since I have a close tie to the subject. Then, I'm sure like last time, she will completely ignore my ideas and go in a different direction. Her plan seems to work, so who am I to be critical.

The flight attendant brings me the best ginger ale I've ever had and I recline my seat and start reading.

I awake from my nap two hours later thinking I've heard my name being called. I glance around and seeing no one familiar, decide I was imagining this, because who would know me on this flight? So I stretch, yawn, and close my eyes again, hoping to catch another forty winks.

"Scott Sawyer."

Okay. That definitely isn't imagined. I pop open an eye, scan first class, and once again see no one familiar or anyone turning their head towards me. This is getting weird.

"Psst."

It came from behind. I turn, and standing there poking her head through the curtains separating the classes is Nancy Law.

"Nancy?" I say, subtly wiping the corners of my mouth, hoping there isn't any drool from my nap.

"In the flesh," she replies cutely. "I thought that was you boarding the plane in L.A."

My gosh. Nancy Law. Probably the sweetest, and I thought, one of the most attractive girls in my high school class. Nothing really stood out about her, it was just the total package of personality and loveliness.

She stands about five seven, has an hour glass figure, great shoulders, dark hair and the warmest brown eyes I've ever seen. And when she smiles her nose still crinkles just a bit. But in my opinion her best facial feature, was always, and still is, that when she smiles, one side of her mouth raises slightly higher than the other. In high school study hall, she would bite that side of her lips often and it just drove me wild. Her parents had moved to Arizona right after our senior year and I hadn't seen her since.

She steps through the curtain and if possible, she looks better in her forties than she did in high school.

The flight attendant notices Nancy now standing in first class and wanders over.

"Can I help you, ma'am?" she asks politely.

"No," Nancy smiles. She places her hand on my shoulder. "I just saw this old fella' I haven't seen since high school and thought I'd say hello."

The flight attendant pulls out her manifest. "You know, Mr. Sawyer, this seat beside you was never booked. I believe I can allow your friend to move up here."

"That would be great," I say, probably a little too enthusiastically. Nancy thanked the young lady and sat down.

In those few seconds, thousands of opening statements rush though my mind but all I can muster is, "You look great." Hey, I'm a writer, not an on the spot speaker. Apparently, this line isn't so bad because I get a really big smile.

"Thank you, Scott. You always were so sweet." She lowers her head as if I have embarrassed her. All through high school, she never seemed to have a clue of how attractive she was and that, of course, made her more attractive.

She raises those amazing eyes and meets mine dead on. "You know, Scott, you have really changed. Honestly, if I hadn't read your books and seen the recent book jacket picture, I might not have recognized you."

Oh, rats. She apparently noticed that my once long blond hair was now shaved and was mostly gray stubble.

"Yeah. After high school I sort of outgrew my hair."

"That's not what I meant," she laughs. "You've changed everywhere, especially in the weight department," she stammers. "You've filled out; in a good way, of course."

"Thank goodness for that," I reply. In school I had always been very thin. In eighth grade I was six feet tall and wrestled in the one hundred twelve pound division. Needless to say, I lost a lot of matches. I gained maybe fifteen or twenty pounds in high school. But now, standing six feet one and weighing around one eighty five, I thought I looked pretty good.

She reaches over my seat and touches my arm. "And you're so tan and fit."

"Well, you can thank the state of Hawaii for that. It's a law. You *have* to be tan and fit if you live there."

"I don't know," she giggles. "I've seen some pretty pasty, physically fit-challenged people over there."

I turn towards her and smile myself. "Those, dear lady, are the tourists." The conversation continues like that for a while, nothing serious, just reminiscing. The flight attendant brings dinner and just as I took a bite of my steak, she drops the idle chit chat.

"Scott," she asks. "Are you happy?"

"Sure," I respond ignorantly. "My steak is great." I glance up and she's biting her lip. "Not what you mean?"

"Not hardly," she shrugs. "I mean…with life. Are you…where you thought you would be at this point?"

I think about that a second, then laugh. "Well, no, not really."

Her eyes widen, then turn sad.

I continue before she gets the wrong idea. "I'm way beyond happy," I explain. "When we were in high school, I figured I would be a teacher or a psychologist, something like that. In a hundred years I, or probably any of my English teachers, would have never thought I would be writing for a living. And, truth be told, I love it. I can't imagine doing anything else."

"And what about your personal life?" she asks.

I put down my fork. "I always hoped that one day I would find someone who loved me as much as I loved them. And I have. I am blessed with a wonderful wife and two great kids."

She glances away. "Sounds like you've got it all."

"For the most part I would have to say that I do."

When she turns back her eyes are moist. "I wish I could say that."

This sounds heavy, so I signal the flight attendant and ask her to take our dishes away and also ask her to bring us both the chocolate cake dessert I noticed on the menu. Hey, if you're going to have a deep conversation, chocolate is a necessity.

"What's up, Nancy?" I ask. She takes a deep breath and begins.

After high school she had gotten a scholarship to Stanford University where she majored in mass communications with an emphasis on television and a minor in journalism. Her junior year, a photography friend of hers asked if she would pose for a project he was doing and somewhere along the line a talent agent had seen the photos and contacted her about doing some modeling and local television ads. She agreed, because it was good money *and it* kept her from having to have a regular job during school.

During her senior year of college she had done her internship with a local television station doing research. One weekend, the female co-anchor had called in with a family emergency and the producer asked Nancy if she would fill in.

"*Just read the copy we give you,*" he had said. "*Piece of cake.*"

And it was. She loved it and the viewers seemingly loved her. The station received over a hundred calls, mostly from guys, asking about the new anchor. Soon she was doing all the weekend news and some morning news. When she graduated, they hired her to be the full time co-anchor of the evening news.

"It was a whirlwind," Nancy says as she licks chocolate icing from her fingers. "But a wonderful whirlwind."

"Sounds great," I say. "So why the tears?"

"Because of my husband, or rather my ex-husband," she sighs, "wasn't as thrilled with my career."

I think about that and am pretty sure of the answer to my next question but ask it anyway. "How could he not have been happy? He had a beautiful, wonderful wife, who I'm sure was pulling down some big bucks. Where's the problem?"

"Well, let's see. His problem was...he had a wife making more money than he was; and, who was working long hours and getting lots of attention."

I sigh, knowing the type. "Where was this guy from?"

"San Francisco."

"Really, I didn't know they had any butt-hole rednecks in California."

She laughs which I take as a good sign and decide to take the conversation in a different direction.

"So...you're on a plane headed to Tennessee..."

She nods. "Yep."

"Visiting or what?"

"A quick visit and possibly an or what." She tells me that she is being courted by a television station in Atlanta. She won't give me the name, but says it's a very big television station based in Atlanta that *specializes* in news. The offer is incredible and she will finally have world wide exposure.

"So," I say. "I'm curious to know what your ex-husband thinks about this."

"Don't have to worry about that anymore. We've been divorced for six months and since we had no kids, I never see him."

"Are you okay with that?"

"Sure. I never got upset about losing him, just about failing at marriage." She looks away, giving me the hint that she doesn't want to say any more on the subject.

"Wow, Nancy. The job sounds great. We'll finally be able to say we have a famous graduate in our high school class."

She shakes her head. "Duh. You're famous."

I shrug. "Nah. I'm just a writer. It's an anonymous fame. You're the only one on this plane who knows who I am."

"Whatever," she says with a grin. "Anyway, I don't have to be in Atlanta until Thursday, so I called Laura and asked if she wanted to get together and go with me."

I have to think for a minute about who Laura could be. Then it hits me. "Laura Anderson?"

"Yep." Nancy and Laura's family had been neighbors since eighth grade. All through school they had been thick as thieves, best friends, co-captains of the high school cheer-leading squad, co-editors of the senior yearbook, and apparently *still* good friends.

"So you guys are still pretty close?"

"We try our best. She tries to come to L.A. a couple of times a year and I get to Tennessee when I can"

"That's great, Nancy."

"Hey. Maybe we can all get together tomorrow or Wednesday."

"Well…"

She notices my hesitation. "Or not."

"It's not that I don't want to, Nancy, and I would love to see Laura…"

"Then what?" she asks.

"I'm going to Tennessee...for a funeral."

The sadness in her eyes returns. "I'm sorry, Scott. Who passed away?"

"A really good friend. You might remember him from school, Jason Maler."

The tears come quickly. She raises her hand to her mouth, then Nancy Law breaks down.

THREE

The flight itself went fairly well. The wheels touched down at Nashville Airport around seven o'clock p.m., Tuesday evening, and my luggage was waiting at the claim area. These days, that's a good flight.

Before landing, I had held Nancy in my arms for at least ten minutes while she cried, all the time wondering why she was so upset. After she composed herself, I asked, and she answered. Turns out she had come back to Tennessee to visit Laura a few years ago and the two of them had run into Jason at a restaurant. A quick romance sparked and soon became a long distance relationship that lasted almost a year before Nancy broke it off. She didn't hear anything more from Jason and then she got married. Now that she was divorced and headed to Tennessee, she had hoped that she could see Jason, apologize, and possibly rekindle that spark from years ago.

We part with a hug at the luggage area and I promise to call her with any news or information. After getting my luggage, I make my way to the car rental counter and am helped by a very nice guy named Skeeter.

"What kind of car would you like?" Skeeter asks.

I think about that a second, reminiscing back to high school days when kids drove cars that had personality, character, recognition. You knew someone by their car and what stickers were on the back window.

I smile as I think about my high school car.

"Mr. Sawyer?" Skeeter says. "What type of car...?"

"I don't guess you have any 1970 snot-colored station wagons?"

Skeeter looks bum-fuddled for a second, then gets it. "That's a joke, right?"

"A nightmare, actually. But I survived."

Skeeter and I decide on a nice Sedan, a BMW convertible actually, not because I'm snotty or arrogant about being wealthy, but because that's all he has left. Apparently, everyone in line before me had rented all of the reasonably priced vehicles. Skeeter sends someone to get the car, and when they pull up in front of the airport I'm pleased because it is a gray 528i, just like the one I have at home. I throw my luggage in the trunk and head out, or so I think. The Nashville Airport has apparently grown and parking lots have been vastly changed, but after three trips around the loading zone I finally find my way out.

I get on Donelson Pike and head over to I-65 South towards Franklin. It's amazing to see the changes that have occurred in the past five years. Progress I guess, but to me, it sure doesn't feel like it. If I didn't know I was going in the right direction, I would assume I'm lost. Nashville, Brentwood and Franklin all seems connected now. There are no longer any farms or large estates separating the towns anymore, just one subdivision or shopping mall after another. It seem the urban sprawl I sought when I left Franklin has finally made it here.

I take the number 65 Franklin exit and find that the same privately owned hotel I remembered from my youth is still there beside Shoney's restaurant. It isn't the Ritz, or the Marriott…okay it's not even really Motel Six, but it has a history. Prom nights, keg parties, poker games…many memories race through my mind as I pull into the parking lot.

I don't know the guy at the front desk but he seems nice and is very helpful. I check in and find my room near the pool. Not bad, really. Cheap, and clean. I laugh as I think about how expensive rooms at this run down old motel would be on Waikiki Beach.

Suddenly, I realize that I still have my phone on silent. When I check, I see there are six messages. I listen and discover five are from Pat wanting to know where I am and the sixth is from Mignonne, just calling to see if I had arrived safely. I call her back and tell her about the long trip, including my run in with Nancy. She understands Nancy's feelings of remorse and regret about Jason and hopes she can find closure. I just can't help but love this woman and her ability to find the best in every situation. We chat briefly about the kids and my plans or rather lack of plans, then after a brief silence, I tell her how much I miss her, love her, and how grateful I am to have her in my life.

The next call is to Pat.

"Where are you?" are the first words out of his mouth. No *hello* or *glad you're safe*.

"I'm in Franklin, just checked in to the hotel."

"I thought I was going to pick you up at the airport."

"I apologize for the change, but I decided I wanted to sight-see a bit and didn't know how available you would be for that." It isn't a complete lie.

"I got ya," Pat says. "Listen, visitation isn't until tomorrow afternoon so I'm thinking we can get together tonight and have dinner. How about it?"

"Sounds good, Pat. Where should I meet you?"

"Are you drinking?" he asks.

"Probably not," I reply. I hadn't been much of a drinker since college. My body just doesn't tolerate it anymore.

"Then come pick me up. I plan on drinking a few to Jason tonight."

I agree, and a few minutes later head off to pick him up. Pat's house is easy to find since it's two blocks from where he grew up. He had explained that his second ex-wife, Reyanne, had originally bought this house, but when they divorced she didn't think she could afford it alone, so he bought it from her. It was small, about fifteen-hundred square feet, with hardly any yard, but Pat wasn't really a house keeper or yard person so it suited him fine. His comment was: as long as there is a big kitchen with a table large enough to get eight poker players around, it's all good.

I pull in his driveway and he's standing there waiting, a beer in his hands.

"You know you could have stayed here," he says as he greets me with a hug.

"I know, but I didn't want to cramp your style just in case you picked up anybody at the funeral."

"Kiss my..." he laughs. "Have you told anyone else you were coming?"

"No," I reply with a shake of my head. "I kind of want to keep it low key. But I did run into someone on the plane." I relay my conversation with Nancy Law.

"Love her heart," is all Pat can muster.

"I know."

He's quiet for a moment, then recovers quickly. "She was so hot in school. How does she look now?"

"Even better."

His eyes grow larger. "Really? You think she'll be at the funeral?"

Pat never changes.

"She was coming in to visit with Laura Anderson for a couple of days." I omit the part about her job interview unsure if that's public knowledge. "She wanted to know what the arrangements are. If time allows, I would guess she would be there."

"I hope so. I would love to see her. You know, I see Laura all the time. She's owns an antique store downtown and sells a lot of things on-line, uses my services a good bit."

He walks around to the passenger door so I guess we're heading out to eat. Pat tells me about a great Cajun place that has opened and he's right on the money. The food and atmosphere are very reminiscent of New Orleans' finest dives and over gumbo and shrimp with grits we catch up.

I knew he had opened a small delivery business a year ago, and he tells me he is still refereeing every high school and church league sport imaginable.

"I'm not getting rich," he says. "But I'm happy and have plenty of time to do what I want." He takes a sip of beer. "No kids, and the ex-wives are all remarried so I don't have that many financial demands." He then updates me on a few of our friends I haven't seen in years, most of whom seemed happy and stable.

The conversation then turns to me. He knows most everything because we do occasionally call or e-mail. He asks about Mignonne and the boys and I assure him everyone was fine when I left, and since I have not heard otherwise I assume all is in order. He's sad Mignonne isn't coming but understands with all she has going on.

I always assumed all of my friends had a crush on Mignonne and I couldn't blame them. I remember specifically at our ten year reunion when all these guys didn't bring dates, hoping to pick up someone at the reunion and of course hadn't. So, the majority of the night they had asked Mignonne to dance with them. At the end of the evening she sat there rubbing her sore feet and told all of them they had better have dates at the twenty year reunion because she wasn't spending that night dancing with all of the losers.

The waitress returns to the table, and as I'm ordering chocolate bread pudding I feel a hand on my back.

"Oh, my stars," comes a sweet southern drawl. "Hey, Pat."

I turn and find myself looking into the beautiful, smiling face of Laura Anderson.

"Hey, Laura," we both answer.

I stand and we embrace in a big hug. After a few seconds, I loosen my grip but she tightened hers and we hold each other for a while longer, no words spoken, just the sound of our breathing and the beating of our hearts. I've noticed that since I've aged, greetings with old acquaintances last longer and I like to think it's because they are either genuinely glad to see me, or because they are simply happy that someone they know is as old as they are. Either way, the hug with Laura is an excellent one. She feels and smells as wonderful as she always did in school.

She raises her head and I see her eyes are wet with tears.

"I'm so glad you're here," she whispers.

"Me too." I glance around the place to find Nancy. "Isn't Nancy with you?"

"No, she's not. She was just a mess after she found out about Jason so I figured I'd come up here and get some food to go."

"I'm so sorry about the way she found out."

"It's Okay, Scott," Laura says reassuringly. "She'll be at visitation tomorrow."

"Good." My chocolate bread pudding arrives and I ask Laura to sit down and join us while she waits on her order. I offer her a spoon to help me eat and she quickly takes it. By this time, Pat has waved over a young lady from the bar and has invited her to join our table. Same old Pat.

It's wonderful as we sit here talking and sharing food, and I'm swept back to wonderful high-school memories. That's when I realize that these next few days will be filled with an abundance of memories, both happy and sad.

I hope I'm prepared.

FOUR

Suddenly, the bird steps forward, lowers his head, and gives a slight peck at my arm. It doesn't hurt, he's just checking me out. Then he raises his slender neck and moves his face within inches of mine. I decide to take a chance. Slowly, I lift my hand from the water and move it towards his head. He ducks slightly, then relaxes, as if to say okay, I pecked you, so now you can pet me. My fingers quiver as I move them closer, then, finally, I touch the brilliant pink feathers. They are as soft, warm, and fuzzy as Mom's old house slippers.

I sit up with a start.

"This is Rock Radio for the rockers who remember."

It's nine o'clock a.m., and the voice from the clock-radio is loud and offensive, not like the DJ's in the seventies who spoke in low gravelly tones and sounded stoned most of the time. I cough and rub my eyes, then reach over and turn off the radio alarm.

It's nine o'clock but feels much earlier. Jet lag. As my feet hit the floor I wonder what caused me to dream about the flamingo. I haven't thought about him or that incredible summer in years. At least I didn't think I had, not until…Jason.

I walk over to the window, push aside the curtains, and am greeted with the sight and sound of traffic on Royal Oaks Boulevard. "Definitely not Hawaii," is all I can say.

All travel magazines should list that the best cure for jet lag has to be a really cold shower with a weak spray, otherwise why would most hotels have them. Surprisingly, though, this hotel shower has great pressure and really hot water, so I forget that best cure and move on to another, a great breakfast followed by a trip through town and maybe the old neighborhood.

The weather forecast on the radio said sunny and seventy five, a typical spring day in Tennessee, so I throw on some khakis and a golf shirt and grab my linen jacket just in case. After seeing the choices at the free breakfast bar, I decide to forego breakfast here and venture to downtown Franklin. Surely with all the progress they had made here someone would have opened an alternative to the greasy spoon that had graced Main Street for nearly a hundred years. Not to say that Jackson's Cafe isn't good, but I'm much older now and my body doesn't react as well to things that can also be used as an engine lubricant.

For the past few years my typical breakfast has consisted of cereal with papaya, guava nectar, and an occasional pineapple turnover if I can sneak it past Mignonne. She's a health nut, always has been. She ran cross country and track in high school and still jogs at least five miles a day. Me, I like walking on the beach, at the leisurely routine of about five miles a week.

I drive downtown and park in the public lot on the north side of town, get out of the car, and decide it's too nice for the jacket. After locking up, I join the other ten or so people walking briskly down Third Avenue towards the square. Laughing, I realize how quick my step is. I haven't walked this fast since moving to Hawaii. Funny how the pace of your walking is the same as the pace of your surroundings. I slow down and let the others race by.

Why rush, I think, then settle into a meander. With my hands in my pockets I casually stroll down the sidewalks and reminisce while glancing at the lines in the concrete I had ridden my bicycle over so many years ago.

I recall the game we played in our neighborhood. It was called, *That Game*, a silly title I know, but it worked. *That game* was a form of bicycle tag and depending on how many kids were playing, you tried to divide into even teams. Most of the time two teams were enough, but occasionally if you had eight kids or more you could make three teams.

The *it* team would then head towards town while the chasers would wait in a neighborhood driveway and count to five-hundred, giving the *it* team time to get to town and hide. After five-hundred, the chasers would head to town as well and try to find the others. To win or swap sides one of the chasers had to physically tag one of the *it* team. The boundaries were the vegetable stand on the Harpeth River, two blocks from the square, and Five Points intersection near the old post office on the other end of Main Street. We usually had enough time to get in two games before the sun started to set. The gang would then grab a snack at Big Star Grocery on Fourth Avenue and talk about the game or the coming movies at the Franklin Cinema.

Simpler times back then. If you were under sixteen, bicycles or your feet were the main modes of transportation and the town was small enough that you could go pretty much anywhere you wanted. Shop keepers were friendly and loved seeing us coming into town because they knew we were good kids and would spend plenty of allowance and lawn-mowing money throughout the summer.

I round the City Hall corner, face the square, and freeze. What's happened? This isn't Franklin. I don't see anything familiar, not a store, a sign, and definitely not a face that I recognize. It's like an episode of The Twilight Zone. I close my eyes and shake my head, thinking maybe I'm having a spell as my grandmother used to say. But when I open them, I conclude I'm not. This is what was happening all over America, small towns growing by leaps and bounds, trying to have a big city feel. Then it hits me…this is what I had longed for Franklin to become and now that it has, I am disappointed.

I start walking again and turn the corner onto Main Street and see about fifteen people who are standing in line outside of a well worn brick building. Above the door hangs a sign that is comfortingly familiar, Jackson's Cafe. Obviously, these people have not heard that grease and cholesterol are bad for you. Or, they are possibly braving heart disease to experience a part of the original Franklin.

The cafe definitely is part of the history of Franklin and you won't find any true local who would deny it. The owner, Clarence Jackson, probably still sells shirts that have, *"Selling grits since the Civil War,"* printed across the front. Jason always said that on the back of the shirt it should read, *"Causing the squirts since the Civil War."* Clarence had flirted with the idea but his partner who was also his wife hadn't seen the humor. That thought of grits and grease brought a warm feeling and I figure *what the heck.*

I join the others in line and stand for maybe a minute when I hear him.

"Oh, Lordy, it can't be true," he says with a big, boisterous voice. "I've got to be seeing things."

The sun is shining directly into my face and without sunglasses I can't see him, but I would know that voice any where.

"Hey, Clarence."

He walks over and wraps his massive, hairy arms around me and squeezes. "Bet you hadn't had a good bear hug from a burly man in a while."

"Not in a while," I gasp as he almost crushes my lungs.

Clarence Jackson is a great guy and loves everyone in town. He is big, robust, and sweet and can talk to anyone about anything and dare anyone to find a subject he doesn't know something about. For years people tried to stump him with remarkable questions about trivia, travel or historical facts, but he always came up with an answer.

In World War II he had served in Africa, Europe, and Japan. After the war, he remained in the service and decided to see the rest of the world at the Army's expense, serving as a cook at many different military bases. After fifteen years of duty and travel, he decided to return to his hometown of Franklin and open a restaurant. From the day the doors first opened, Jackson's Cafe was a success. Clarence spent most of his waking hours there, loving the work and the people. And the people loved him back, especially when he would share his life's adventures, filled with action, humor, and romance. He had more stories about people, places, and things than I had ever heard from any living person.

Many people suggested he write a book. In fact, I had suggested it about five years ago, but his standard answer had always been, "I never liked reading, so why would I make someone else do it."

Occasionally, we doubted the validity of a few of his tales, because if the dates of his stories were correct, he had to be somewhere in the vicinity of one-hundred and forty years old.

However, there were, as there always are, a few people who didn't like Clarence. They thought he was arrogant with his made up tales and somewhat greedy with the prices he charged at the restaurant. But the truth was, those people were jealous competitors who griped because no one ate at their restaurants. Clarence was one of the best people I had ever known. He always had a job for any kid that needed one; helped any charity that called; and always brought food to the funeral home when someone died.

A few years ago, my dad told me he had heard a rumor that Clarence had written in his will that Jackson's Cafe was to be left to the city of Franklin and that he was leaving enough money to keep it running indefinitely with all profits to be divided between the two city high schools.

"Dad-gummit, boy!" he shouts with a hearty slap on my back. "It sure is good to see you."

After regaining my balance, I reach out my hand and we shake. "Thanks, Clarence, I'm glad to see someone I know."

"There's plenty of people you know inside, boy." A somber look suddenly appears across his face. "I take it you're here for Jason's funeral?"

I nod.

"Well," he says as he scratches his head. "Come on in and let's get you somethin' to eat. Then we'll talk about it."

A few people whined and complained as Clarence led me past them to the door, but I didn't care. I bet most of them are tourists and the rest have only lived here a while.

As he pushes the door ajar he shouts, "Look here, Mona. Look who I brought ya!" Ms. Mona is Clarence's second and current wife.

His first wife, Akiko, was, according to him, a beautiful eighteen year old Japanese girl he had rescued during the clean up mission after the war ended. She was a farmer's daughter who had lost both parents and two brothers to the war. Somehow, Clarence had convinced his company commander to let her travel with the unit until they could find somewhere safe for her to stay. They never found a suitable place, as Clarence put it, so he decided the safest thing would be for her to marry him and come to America. The Army frowned on this and for months kept pushing back the paperwork for the marriage license, hoping he would change his mind. But that didn't happen. His love and admiration just grew stronger and finally, six months later, they were married. He then wrote his parents about his bride and was disappointed to find they weren't thrilled or that no one in the family or town would be. He was devastated and decided to stay overseas and just keep traveling, hopeful that the discrimination would soon fade now that the war had ended. Sadly, Akiko never got to America.

She died of breast cancer the day after their fifteenth wedding anniversary. He took her back to Japan and had her buried with her family. Then, Clarence Jackson hopped on a ship, and sailed home.

Several years later, in the early seventies, Mona Wilkes walked into his life. She was from Abilene, Texas and had hitchhiked to Nashville hoping to become a country music singer and get on the Grand Ole Opry. A producer on Music Row was encouraging but told her she needed to hone her skills as a singer and songwriter, and the best way to do that was to find a place to perform. He then gave her a list of honky-tonks around town and wished her luck. She struck out in all of the places on Music Row, no one wanting to give her a shot, but then she came to the last name on her list, Jackson's Café, owner, Clarence Jackson. She didn't know where Franklin was but the sign at the bus station had it listed so she climbed aboard. The bus from Nashville to Franklin dropped her off right in front of Jackson's Cafe. Clarence immediately noticed the cowboy hat and tight ruffled shirt through the window and fell in love with her the moment she walked through the door.

I asked him once how he knew she was the one. His reply was simple.

"She was big and buxom and had blond hair down to her hind parts," he had said with a smile, "and I just knew that she was it."

He then built a small stage area beside the counter so she could sing when she wasn't waiting on customers. It was always said that she had a pretty good voice but after she and Clarence fell in love, she knew that he wouldn't sell the restaurant and follow her on the road so she traded her dream of fame for a dream of love.

"Oh, my stars," she gushes as she rushes to the counter and grabs me. She could hug almost as tightly as Clarence but her big cushiony chest made the hug much more pleasant.

"Hey, Ms. Mona."

She pushes me to arm's length. "Let me get a look at ya." She runs her eyes up and down my body and I know what's coming. "Mercy, child. You're just wasted down to nothin'. Don't y'all eat over there in Hawaii?"

"Yes, Ma'am. Sometimes I even eat three meals a day."

"Psshh," she hisses. "I bet it's all grilled food or, Heaven forbid, steamed."

"Most of the time, yes," I answer as if I should be ashamed.

"Honey, you know fish ain't no good for you unless it's fried." She squeezes my arm. "The fryin' is what kills all the mercury in the fish."

Clarence mercifully separates us and says," Get on back in the kitchen, Hon, and bring this boy somethin' edible."

She shakes her head and points her chubby finger at me. "I told you that you shouldn't marry any girl that enjoyed joggin' as much as that Mignonne girl does." With that statement she saunters off but I know differently.

Mona always loved Mig and had actually served us a huge piece of chocolate meringue pie on our first date. We had ordered two pieces, yet she brought us one big slice with two forks along with the sentiment, *If you're gonna share kisses, you can surely share pie.*

It's a line we can't wait to use on our boys and their dates one day.

Clarence motions for me to sit at the counter while he re-heats everyone's coffee. I spin around on the barstool and scan the crowd for familiar faces. A couple of people wave. I recognize them as friends of my parents. They come over and talk for a moment, wanting to know about the family and my life in the islands. Several others then come up and say hello. Some I know; others I think I should know, but can't remember for sure. Most of the others hear my name and are just fans of my books.

For a very brief moment I'm the local celebrity come home, and that fame lasts all of seventeen minutes and involves maybe eleven people. This is a wonderful characteristic of the small town that hadn't changed. Over the years many celebrities have moved to Franklin, but after a while they just become your neighbors and are part of daily life. Some appreciate that quality, and others don't. The *don'ts* usually move to California or New York, where they will get the proper recognition and appreciation, and what's funny is…no one ever seems to miss them.

After chatting up a few new customers, Clarence returns to the counter, pours me a cup of his self-titled famous coffee. He then sits and leans in towards me. "When did you get to town?" he asks, a toothpick dangling from his lower lip.

"Last night," I reply as I nervously take a sip of the muddy brew before me. I never have been much of a coffee drinker and the few times I do drink the stuff, it has to be Kona coffee from Hawaii. I cough and try not to gag as the black acid scorches my throat.

Clarence laughs and replaces my mug with a glass of orange juice. "Just playin' with ya. I know you don't appreciate my brew."

I drink half the orange juice in one swallow to quell the fire and remove some of the coffee taste out of my mouth. "I got in around six."

He pulls the toothpick free and points it at me. "You good with a place to stay?"

"Yes, Clarence. I'm fine."

He grunts, replaces the toothpick between his teeth, then turns to pour his own mug of joe. "So how'd you hear about Jason?"

"Pat called."

"Figured as much. I called him this morning, around six-thirty, figured he'd know visitation times. Some gal answered. I made her wake him up and talk to me. But the stinker didn't say a word about you bein' here."

"We had dinner last night and saw Laura Anderson," I chuckle. "But after Laura left, he and *that gal* started shooting tequila. I dropped them off at his place then drove my rental car back to my motel. To be perfectly honest, I'm not sure he even remembers I'm in town."

"Oh," Clarence winked. "I remember nights like that!"

We both laugh and continue talking when he isn't helping Mona in the kitchen. Watching them together is a real testimony to what love is all about, her playful griping while working and him occasionally swatting her behind when she passes by. Every few swats she stops and kisses him, then shoos him back out of the kitchen with the words, "Get out yonder and do somethin' useful."

FIVE

Horribly stuffed from three fried eggs, two strips of bacon, a bowl of grits with cheese, and a piece of toast just for the heck of it, I waddle out of Jackson's Cafe. Half-heartedly, I curse myself for allowing Clarence and Ms. Mona to stuff me silly, but really it was probably the best country breakfast I've eaten since my Grandmother died ten years ago.

I stretch a bit, then decide to continue my stroll through town at an even slower pace due to my full belly. The Franklin Square has always been one of your better small town squares with its Civil War monument and seasonal landscaping, but as I admire the structure and historic value, I have to admit that now I found it down right beautiful, full of tulips, grass, and flowering shrubs. Funny how I never truly appreciated it before.

I cross the street, dodging several delivery trucks and step up on the greenest grass I have set foot on since leaving the mainland. Nowhere in Hawaii do they have luscious grass like this. I sit on one of the wooden benches placed on the square in memory of a loved one and glance around. No one is really paying me any mind so I slip off my shoes and socks and walk across the prickly green carpet. It feels so wonderful on my feet that I make a few fists with my toes and scrunch the blades of grass. This feeling reminds me of one particular memory from my youth. One summer at Vacation Bible School, I was probably ten, our teacher asked what each of us thought Heaven might be like. My reply was simple, *walking barefoot across a freshly mowed field on a cool summer evening.*

Suddenly, another memory comes as a flash.

* * *

The flamingo lowered his head again allowing his eyes to meet mine. Like statues, we stayed, staring deep into each others eyes. In that quiet, still moment, it was like our minds melded, causing me to feel his calmness and contentment and he my curiosity and wonder.

* * *

A shiver shakes my body. The flamingo again, summer of seventy-eight. I was fifteen years old and already feeling that I wanted more from life than any small town could offer. The bright lights and fast action of a big city held the ultimate appeal of progress and adventure. How could a kid be so drawn to a life he had never experienced and had only seen on television or read about in magazines? But I had been through big cities before, St. Louis, Kansas City, Denver, and loved the idea of living there.

A few summers earlier we had taken a family vacation out west. For three weeks my brother and I were cooped up in the rear facing back seat of the snot colored station wagon. Our view, the front of the pop-up camper we were towing. In the middle row sat the cooler and snacks. There was no air conditioning and only A.M. radio which couldn't pick up any signals crossing the flat plains of Kansas and Oklahoma. My brother, Tim, and I griped about the lack of technology, but really didn't mind so much. My mom always found ways to keep us entertained; the license plate game, car bingo, comic books.

We stayed mostly in state or national parks which meant no bath houses, no hot water, and definitely no amenities like a pool or arcade. But that was a time when kids played outside as long as there was daylight, and going two or three days without a real bath bothered no one under the age of twelve. Tim and I had explored more places and played more *army* and *cowboys and Indians* that summer than I ever remember at any other time of my life.

We look back now and can't imagine how we survived those summer family expeditions with hardly any money and nothing but love and togetherness. But to be truly honest, those were some of the best times of my life, and I would love to repeat each and every one of those trips with my wife and kids.

I hear some giggling behind me, turn and see three little girls who have also taken off their shoes and socks and are playing in the grass as well. A woman I figure has to be their Mom is reading a book, one of mine actually, and seems to be completely indifferent to my presence. My picture is right there on the back cover jacket and I'm standing fifteen feet away but there is no recognition whatsoever. Once again, I appreciate the wonderful anonymity of being a writer.

I glance toward my shoes still under the bench where she is now sitting and notice that she also had slipped off her shoes. I go over and ask if I can sit beside her while I put my shoes on and she says sure.

"Good book?" I ask deciding to have a little fun.

"Yeah, it's okay," she responds coolly. "But I like this author's wife's book better."

So much for her getting an autograph from me. "Well," I say. "Enjoy your day." I wave to the kids and head on down the street.

Five Points intersection is on the eastern end of the Main Street block, pretty much where downtown ends. When I was little, from the Square to Five Points were the best two blocks of town, housing the Franklin Cinema, Book and Hobby Shop, Co-Op Barber Shop, Jim's Pool Hall, and Western Auto. Western Auto was a hardware store that sold everything—bicycles, sporting goods, and tools. So naturally, all of us kids hung out there. The owner didn't mind at all. We didn't spend a lot of money but we were always good for a baseball or sack of marbles.

The Book and Hobby Shop was comic book and magazine central and the owner didn't mind if we caught up on magazines and comics as long as we didn't sit on the floor and make a day of it. They also carried the coolest selection of Matchbox and Hot Wheels cars, as well as model airplanes and art supplies.

None of those stores exists any longer and most aren't even remembered by the people who now call themselves locals. There *is* a book store but there's nothing comfortable or down home about it. I figure my books fetch a hefty price in there compared to the cost cutter prices of discount and large retail stores, which means more royalties for me, but that fact doesn't appeal to me so I choose not to enter.

Walking a little further, I come to the movie theater. The Franklin Cinema had opened and closed at least four times during my childhood, but when it was open, you could find most of Franklin, especially the kids, crammed into the dark theater sharing popcorn and whispering to each other about who was sitting with whom.

According to the signs in the window, it's closed again. Another sign says, *Save the Historic Franklin Cinema,* and is asking for donations. Maybe I can help, but then again, sometimes it's just time to let go. There's a huge multiplex near the mall which is more appealing to young people and more convenient to shoppers.

I slowly turn, a bit sad about the reality of progress, then glance up and down the street and realize that, in fact, I don't recognize any of the stores, shops, or restaurants. Even the corner drug store is gone, replaced by the well-known monster coffee house that occupies so many corners of America and charges more for an individual cup of coffee than Jackson's Cafe charges for an entire meal.

The Presbyterian Church thankfully *still* graces the corner of Fifth Avenue and has since before the Civil War. At least something is familiar.

How disheartening it feels to realize that my hometown wasn't really mine anymore. No longer is there the warmth or character I felt so comfortable with, nor the intimacy or friendliness of the people who own the businesses. No longer is the security of thinking that nothing will ever change.

Then I remember that was the very reason I left.

SIX

Hi. This is Mignonne. Sorry I can't take your call right now. Please leave a message and I will get back to you as quickly as possible.

"Hey. I was just calling to tell you I miss you, and to let you know that I have entered some type of other dimension. Franklin is no longer Franklin and I feel like a foreigner in my old hometown. How's that for irony. At least Jackson's Café is still here. Clarence and Mona say hello." I sit there a moment, not sure what else to say so I just say what I feel. "I love you."

I flip the phone closed, figuring she must be in the shower or hasn't turned on her phone yet. It's around six-thirty back on the island, so she and the kids will just be starting their day.

I walk around a couple more blocks to see what else has changed but after strolling through a few church yards and alleys, I decide I've re-lived all of the nostalgia I can handle for one morning. Glancing at my watch I see that I've piddled away most of the morning. It's almost noon and the lunch time crowd is descending on Main Street's fancy pubs and bistros, but I know I'd have no appetite until much later in the day, if at all.

I should probably call Pat, but figure if he wants to find me he'll call. My guess is he's still in bed nursing a hangover or entertaining his overnight guest.

Heading back towards the parking lot and my car, I decide to alter my route a bit and go down Fourth Avenue to see what's happened to the historic homes. I'm betting most of them have been turned into offices or antique stores.

A gentle breeze wisps across me as if blowing the past. I close my eyes and breathe in the southern air, then cough profusely as I catch a whiff of the garbage truck passing by.

Continuing down the sidewalk, I'm amazed and impressed at how beautifully the houses are decorated for spring. Tulips, buttercups, and Easter themed displays are abundant as far as the eye can see. Some of the houses have, indeed, become offices and a few are advertised as recording studios, but most of them have kept their hominess.

"Excuse me." The voice comes from behind and isn't very loud, so I figure they're not talking to me and keep walking. "Excuse me, Scott?"

Well, can't ignore that, so I turn and find a lovely young woman standing there.

"Scott Sawyer?" she asks.

"Yes…" I extend my hand. "And you are?"

"Lucinda Evans." Her hand is extremely soft, but her handshake is very firm. She's of Asian descent, yet tall, has beautiful skin, and seems to be in her early thirties. She also has the most incredible blue eyes.

"Lucinda," I say with a smile while still holding her hand. "Lovely name. Do we know each other? I know some Evans in town but…"

"But I don't quite look like any of them?" she smiles.

"Right," I say. "You're much prettier." I release her hand and she blushes. "You from around here, Lucinda?"

"Dad was. Mom, obviously wasn't."

"Who's your father?"

"Harold Evans."

I don't recognize the name but figure my parents would know him.

"He and my mom, Hiroko, met and married in Tokyo. My father was a tall, handsome, corporate pilot, with a sexy southern accent, and impossible to resist azure eyes." She points to her own eyes. "Mom was a petite, adventure seeking, Japanese woman who sought change and excitement. He flew for a company based in Japan and loved it there. They met at a golf tournament and were married after only six weeks of courting. Three years after, I was born."

"Sounds like your mom and dad both got an adventure."

"Yes," she nods, "and then some. Sadly, he died of a heart attack when I was eight."

"I'm sorry."

"Don't be," she shrugs. "I feel I had a lifetime with my dad in those eight years. He was the most loving and attentive father I can imagine and every minute we shared was an adventure for me. We experienced so much, but the thing I remember most are the stories he told about Tennessee and of course, Franklin. So, when I was ten, Mom said she wanted to move here and let me experience some of my Father's heritage, so we did. Later I discovered her family had pretty much disowned her for marrying an American and it ticked off my mom so much she wanted to get me away from that kind of mind set."

"Did the family ever reconcile with her?"

"Yes, about five years ago her brother came over, apologized for the family's behavior, and invited her to return. She did and is still living there."

"And you decided to stay."

"I can't imagine living anywhere else. My father's family and the town of Franklin accepted us into their hearts and never made us feel like we didn't belong. It's a special place and will hopefully always be my home."

"Wow. That's a great story," I say. "Being from Franklin I'm always amazed at what brings people here from so far away."

"Well, being from here, you should know."

I nod. "So, Lucinda. How do you know me?"

"Oh, I'm sorry. I saw you through the window," she says, pointing to a large bay window on the front of the white house behind us. "Recognized you from your book jacket. I'm a big fan. Of course, I guess everyone around here is a big fan."

I ignore her last statement. "And what do you do, Lucinda?"

"I am an attorney and this house is my office."

"Nice," I say, quite impressed. "You must do very well. What type of attorney are you?"

Her eyes glance downward, then back up and lock on mine. There's a sadness that wasn't there before.

"Actually, Scott," she explains. "I'm Jason Maler's attorney and I'm representing his estate."

"Oh...right..." I stammer.

"Pat called and told me you were coming in. I guess you know about the note the police found on Jason.

I had almost forgotten. Some friend I was. "It was about a letter, right?"

"Right." She paused, then continued. "Have you spoken with Sherry?"

"No," I whisper.

"I thought maybe you had and were looking for my office."

"Uh, no, actually, I was just walking around," I say. "I haven't been here in a while and was getting my bearings."

"Oh...oh, okay," she says. "Well, I won't keep you. We can talk later." With a slight wave she turns to walk away, then stops and turned around.

"Lucinda?"

She turns back towards me. "Yes."

I try to speak, to ask about Jason, but my throat feels like it's closed up on me.

She walks over and takes my hand. "Jason and I had become really good friends over the past few years. I met him after I bought this house and started remodeling. We got along immediately because we had so much in common. He worked so hard to help me put the place together. He was an incredible man and I loved him very much"

I squeeze her hand. "Thank you for telling me that."

She raises her azure eyes to mine, so beautiful, but brimming with tears.

"So, you guys were a couple?" I ask.

She lets go of my hand and hooks her arm in mine. "Please come in." We move towards the house and when we reach the porch she stops. "I would have gladly dated him, but he didn't think of me that way. I believe I was more like a sister to him, especially after his real sister, Mary, moved away. He watched out for me, sent me clients, checked out the guys I did date."

She glances away, towards the tulip garden where an angel fountain sprays its plume into the sun which causes a small rainbow. I notice she's smiling, as if seeing someone familiar.

"I feel his spirit here," she says. "In the gardens...the house. We had dinner here just hours before..." Her eyes drop to the porch steps. "He told me things had gotten worse. And at that point, I was the only one who knew about..." she hesitates as if wanting me to finish her sentence.

"About what?" I ask.

She bites her lower lip, looking as if she's said too much. "Come with me."

"Wow!" I gasp as I enter through the front door. The foyer is three stories tall with a grand crystal chandelier. The light cascading through the front picture window strikes the dangling glass shards, causing winks of light to scurry across the walls like glistening fairies. An amazing spiral staircase rises to the second floor, merges into a large landing, then continues its climb to the third story. The floors are burled walnut with a finish so stunningly clear that it seems you could reach your hand into the wood and touch the rings.

"Awesome," I say as I walk over to the staircase and stroke the hand carved rail. "Who did all this?" I ask, figuring some master craftsman must have flown in from Germany, Switzerland, maybe Russia.

"Jason." She walks into the next room leaving me stunned, amazed, and genuinely confused.

I follow. "Jason did all of this?"

"Oh, I helped a bit with paint and wallpaper," she says as she moves to a file cabinet. "But all of the wood work, floors, custom painting...he did it all." She pulls open a drawer, removes a file, and goes to her desk. "Please sit, Scott."

I do so, still glancing around at the remarkable artistry.

"What did you mean earlier, that you were the only one who knew?"

She ignores my question and opens the file, then pulls out a manilla envelope. "This is what Jason wished me to give to you. I have not seen its contents and it's none of my business unless you want to share it with me. He was of sound body and mind when he gave me this as part of his final bequests." She hands it to me.

Once I take it, she continues.

"That concludes our business *for now*, Scott." She leans forward and folds her hands on the desk. "I hope to see you again when things have become more clear."

"I'd like that, Lucinda." I place my finger on the envelope's seal and began to tear.

"Scott," she says.

I stop.

"Not here. This is something special. He told me that he wanted you to open it at a particular place."

"Where?"

She shakes her head. "He never told me."

I stare at the envelope, wondering.

Lucinda stands, walks around the desk, and sits on the corner. "He said you would know."

I raise my eyes and for the first time noticed the painting behind and above her desk. It's a watercolor, about three foot by five foot, lush woods, a river, a pond, and…flamingoes. I glance to the corner of the canvas, J.M.

SEVEN

I sit in my rental car staring at the manilla envelope in the seat next to me and wonder...about Lucinda...the house...and the painting, but mostly about what Jason has told Lucinda. *"A special place,"* she said. *"He said that you would know."*

The truth was, I did know, but I wasn't sure if I was ready to go there yet, especially since I had no idea what this envelope contained. My visit with Lucinda was somewhat enlightening, but also left me with many questions. When had Jason become a carpenter and craftsman? When had he become such an amazing artist? And why had he never shared any of it with me?

I turn the key and the BMW comes alive. It's such a beautiful spring day and the road beckons for me to put the convertible top down and head down the highway, but to where? The answer comes easily. Hoping roads hadn't changed too much, I turn left onto Third Avenue, circle the Square, then head west on Main Street. After turning right at 5th Avenue, I go two blocks, then turn left onto Highway 96 West.

When I left Franklin years ago, there was a McDonalds, a couple of banks, and a barbecue joint near the main intersection. Now there are car dealerships, schools, and subdivisions on both sides of the road. This stretch of road connecting Franklin and Fairview was always *supposed* to be the next sprawl of urban development, and I guess that finally happened.

The highway is very straight and flat and many weekend nights during high school, we brought Jason's Camaro out here and opened her up, sometimes pushing the speedometer to one hundred miles an hour. We never thought about the consequences if a cop were to suddenly appear or if a deer unexpectedly ran across the road. We weren't any different from most kids, young and stupid.

I hope my kids have more common sense than I had back then. I wonder if that's what Jason was searching for the night he crashed the car, if he was trying to reach that euphoria of being young and carefree once again? But why, when he seemed to have so much going for him?

As I glance from side to side, it dawns on me that I was five miles from town and there is no open pasture land, woods or ponds visible anymore. There's just an endless parade of brick, concrete, and siding…cookie cutter million dollar homes on practically zero lot lines. What were these people thinking?

Up ahead is a familiar site, a blinking light at the intersection of Highway 96 and Old Hillsboro Road. I smile as I remember the fall of 1979 and spring of 1980, when I had made the turn onto Old Hillsboro Road on so many Friday and Saturday nights to pick up my high school girlfriend, Melanie.

But instead of turning, I continue past the intersection about a mile further and turn right into the subdivision, Forest Home Farms, where I am surprised at the number of homes now occupying the area. There are so many new houses that I have difficulty finding the quiet cul-de-sac where so many late weekend nights were spent parking.

Melanie had actually found the secluded spot while she was in Driver's Ed class. At that time, they had just started developing this part of the subdivision and had poured the streets and cul-de-sacs, but no houses were under construction and there were no street lights yet, so the place was pitch black. She lived just a few miles down the road, so we could park here and take advantage of every wonderful minute before curfew came.

Many beautiful, starry nights we'd climb into the hatchback of my old Mustang II, make out, and proclaim our true love for one another. Sometimes the windows would get so steamy we could write on them and more than once she drew a little heart with our initials, M.F and S.S. Then she always drew an arrow made from the word love. Other nights we'd just sit on the hood of the car and hold each other while looking at the stars and imagine our future together, yet knowing full well with heart breaking certainty that we probably wouldn't end up together.

I pull into the cul-de-sac, but there are so many cars on the street it's difficult to find a place to pull in so I don't. Instead, I drive a bit further and pull into the parking lot of a park area that has one of those huge wooden play-sets. Beside the playground there are picnic tables near where we used to park.

I decide to get out of the car and walk around and, when I do, I see that a few of the moms sitting at the tables have noticed me. I don't think of myself as looking like a threat, but in today's world of stalkers and kidnappings I figure it's better to put unsure minds at ease.

"Good morning," I call out with a wave, completely ignoring the playing children and focusing solely on the moms. A redhead who I figure must be the leader of this mid-day play group waves back. She and a brunette are sitting together on one side of the picnic table while another brunette sits across from them. A small cooler is her companion.

"Good morning, yourself," the redhead says with a giggle. "How are you today?"

"Excellent. And you ladies. How are you today?"

"Wonderful. The kids are playing nicely and…" She raises her glass. "And we have drinks."

"Sounds like you are having a good morning."

"Care to join us?" she asks.

"Thank, you." Ah, Southern hospitality. The closest I've ever come to it anywhere else is in Hawaii. "You sure you don't mind?"

"Not at all," she replies. The brunettes don't seem so sure.

I sit on the other side of the cooler and before I can introduce myself, the interrogation begins.

"You new to the neighborhood?" the redhead asks, "Or just looking around?"

I give one of my most charming smiles and wonder if I should run. "Actually, neither." I hear the unzipping of the cooler behind me. I hope they don't have a tazer gun or pepper spray in there. Kind of sounds like one of my novels. Maybe not.

"Bloody Mary? Mimosa?" The brunette beside me asks.

"No thanks."

She proceeds to pull out a small bottle of vodka and a can of V-8. I also see a small bottle of champagne and a bottle of orange juice in the cooler.

"You're quite prepared," I comment.

"I have six kids," she says as she makes her Bloody Mary. "The only reason my husband is still alive is because I drink."

"Enough said."

She laughs and actually begins to snort.

That's when I realize she's a bit tipsy. Hey. It is like one of my novels.

"Come on. Have a drink with us," the other brunette says.

"Sorry, ladies. I'm still on Hawaiian time so that puts it at around eight in the morning for me."

"You *are* him," the brunette beside the redhead gasps. "I told you, Julie," she says to the redhead.

"Told her what?" I ask naively.

The three of them burst out laughing.

"Sorry, Scott," the bartender says.

"So you know me…"

The redhead introduces herself first. "I'm Julie."

"A pleasure," I respond.

"Dawn," the brunette beside her says.

"Hey, Dawn."

I turn to the brunette guarding the cooler. "And you are?"

"Holly Cooper."

"So, do you girls always invite strange guys to join you at playtime?"

"You don't really think we'd be this forward with a stranger, do you?" Dawn asks. "Well," she reconsiders with a laugh. "Julie might."

Julie glares at Dawn, then smiles at me. "We don't get many guys coming to the playground in the middle of the day, so, of course, we noticed you. Then Holly thought she recognized you. Dawn believed her, but I didn't."

I glance at Holly. "So how did you recognize me?"

"We always meet up here every day with the kids and a few months ago decided to start a discussion session."

"And what do you discuss?"

"All sorts of things," Julie chimes in. "Movies, dating…"

"Books," Dawn adds.

"Right." Back to Holly. "And last week our book discussion was about your latest novel."

This seems promising. "So was it a good discussion?"

"I liked it," Dawn raises her hand.

I turn to Julie. "What did you think?"

She shrugs. "It was a fun read."

I raise my eyes to Holly. "Well?"

"Sorry," She bites her lip. "A bit too much fluff. I actually liked your wife's book better."

I'm starting to see a theme here. "Well. I'll be sure to tell her."

Dawn leans a bit closer. "Hey, Scott. I got a question."

"Shoot."

"Do you make up everything in your books or is it based on…" she rolls her eyes.

I'm lost.

"She wants to know if the sex is real," Julie says matter-of-factly.

"Thanks, Julie," Dawn hisses. "It's not just the sex. I just always wonder if the relationships are based on real relationships or maybe relationships you wish you had?"

"That's a very good question, Dawn," I say. "Actually, most of the women and relationships in my books are an amalgam, a combination of one or more people and events that occurred in my life."

Dawn sighs. "Not quite the romantic answer I was looking for."

"Sorry, Dawn."

"I don't know," Holly says. "That relationship in his first book was pretty intense."

"I didn't think you really liked his books that much?" Julie said.

"Shut up, Julie."

I can't help but laugh. "Holly, you've nailed me. The relationship in that book *was* real."

"Really," Holly smiles. "How long ago?"

"High school. And you probably won't believe this, but she and I used to go parking on this very cul-de-sac right here."

"No way," Julie gasps.

"Way," I reply. "We'd park just over there, crack the windows, and make out to great songs like, *Still*, by the Commodores, *Babe*, by Styx, and *Always and forever*, by Heatwave."

"Hey. Wasn't there a poem or song you made reference to in your first book?" Dawn asked. "I remember one playing in the movie."

I still remember the words like I was seventeen again. "The song is called, *Thank You*, by Led Zeppelin."

Julie shrugs. "Who would have thought something so pretty could have come from a rock band like that?"

"*The* rock band," I say. "Ladies. It's been wonderful meeting you, but I've got to get going."

"Hey," Dawn says. "You never said why you came out here."

I think about making something up but these ladies have been very up front and honest with me. "I'm in town for the funeral of a friend."

All three sets of eyes lower to the table.

"Sorry," says Dawn. "I wasn't trying to be nosey."

"It's fine, Dawn. The truth is, I haven't been to Tennessee for a while and I'm seeing a lot of people and places I haven't seen in a long time, so I'm feeling a bit nostalgic, and thought I would visit some places that held happy memories like this one." I seemed to have killed the happy mood, so it's definitely time to go.

"Who was your friend?" Julie asks. "Anyone we would know?"

None of these women seem to be much over thirty so I can't imagine any of them knowing Jason. "His name's Jason Maler."

"The artist," Holly says matter-of-factly. "I read about that in the paper. Wow. You guys must have been really close for you to come in from Hawaii."

"Very close." I decide to leave out the fact that I haven't seen or spoken to him in years.

"I must have missed it," Julie says. "What artist?"

"You know," says Holly. "He did the painting in our sun-room that you like so much?"

"The flamingoes? Oh my gosh I do love that painting. Didn't I meet him once?"

"Yeah, you met him one time at our summer party," Holly answers. "He came with that lawyer, Lucinda, who knows Seth."

"Seth?" I ask.

My husband," Holly explains.

The ladies then launch into a discussion about this party and the painting and I decide to leave. The conversation about Jason's art is one that I will not be able to contribute to. I get hugs and best wishes from each lady and Holly gives me her address after I promise that I will send an autographed copy of my wife's next book.

I climb back into the BMW and take in my surroundings. It wasn't quite the moment of memories I had hoped for, but it was nice time well spent with three women who suddenly didn't seem like strangers because they actually knew who Jason was.

I start the car, then turn on the XM radio and tune it to the all Led Zeppelin channel, hoping that just maybe I'll get lucky and *Thank You* will be playing.

Melanie and I broke up in late spring of 1980 and like most high school relationships, seeing each other in the school halls was awkward at first, but time soon removed those uncomfortable feelings and we became friends again, and close friends we still remain. She moved to Virginia after college and marriage but we still keep in touch, mostly through e-mail and Christmas cards.

It would be nice to see each other more often than we do, but it's okay that we only see each other occasionally. Because I am always comforted by the fact that I know she is always there if I need her and she knows the same about me.

Doubting she will be at Jason's funeral and wondering if she has even heard about him, I make a mental note to e-mail her when I get back to the hotel.

I then put the car in gear and drive away to Robert Plant singing *Kashmir*. As I pull away, I glance once more at the cul-de-sac, send Melanie a sweet thought with my mind, and wonder what she is doing at this very moment.

EIGHT

I'm two miles from town when my cell rings.

"Scott Sawyer," I reply in business mode.

"Hey, It's Pat."

"Hey."

"Where are you?"

"A couple of miles out of town."

"Why?"

A good question. "Oh, just seeing the sights. I had breakfast at Clarence's."

"Oh, Lord," Pat sighs. "That old coot called this morning, woke me up a the crack of dawn."

"That's what he said."

"So where exactly are you?" Pat asks.

"After breakfast I walked around town a bit, then decided to take a drive out to Old Hillsboro Road, see how it's changed."

"Isn't that where you and Melanie used to hang out?"

"Yeah."

Pat laughs. "Wasn't that where you got egged on Halloween?"

"You should know since you and Jason were the ones who egged me."

He continues laughing. "I swear it wasn't us, but I would have liked to have seen the expressions on your faces."

I chuckle myself as I remember that night.

* * *

Halloween 1979

Melanie and I had been to dinner and a haunted house, then decided to spend some quality alone time before I met up with the guys to get into some Halloween mischief. She and I were staring deeply into each others eyes and had just started kissing when *SPLAT*, six eggs smacked into the windshield. By the time I got out of the car, the culprits had sped away, but I could hear them laughing all the way down the road. It was so dark I couldn't make out the car, but the loud muffler pipes sounded very similar to those on a certain 1972 Camaro.

I checked out the windshield and hood for damage and was panicked to see the pulverized eggs dripping towards the paint. With great sadness and a big apology, I told Melanie that I had to get the car to the car-wash or Dad would be very ill with me. She said she understood, but told me that I owed her big time for cutting our date short. I promised that I would make up for it and when I walked her to her door, she let me off with a smile and one of the best kisses I'd ever had, wanting me to know what I was going to miss. After I got in the car I glanced back towards the door and saw her laughing.

Then it was off to the car wash, where I sprayed the car several times until there was no trace of yolk anywhere. Then I went on a search for the culprits. Turns out I didn't have to travel far. The two of them were sitting on my front porch.

I pulled in and decided to play it cool.

"Hey, guys," I said casually as I walked over and placed my hand on the Camaro's hood. "Engine's kind of warm. Y'all just get here?"

They exchanged quick glances.

"No," Jason shrugged. "We've been here a while."

"Yeah. You told us to be here at nine," Pat added.

I checked my watch, nine-ten. Maybe it wasn't them.

We got in the car and I saw they were loaded for bear. On the floorboard was a cooler of water balloons and next to me were two cases of toilet paper. It was a beautiful warm October night, so Jason had both windows rolled down and the radio blasting. That was during his Village People days, a time that Pat and I were embarrassed by, but you couldn't help but get tickled when big bodybuilder, Jason, started doing the Y.M.C.A. dance.

Our first stop was in a subdivision close to where Jason lived. Two girls we knew lived there, and we felt they needed the popularity status of being rolled by us guys. It was an incredibly easy and convenient job because they lived next door to each other and had huge trees in their yards.

Our plan was to go with the pastel toilet paper in one yard and the two ply patterned paper in the other. After 57 rolls, Jason and I were admiring our handiwork when we heard Pat.

"Psst."

We looked around but couldn't see him.

"Over here."

I followed the sound of his voice and saw his shadowed outline on the porch across the street. We wandered over and crept to the porch.

"Look at this," Pat said. In the rocking chair sat a dummy, a very human looking dummy. "I'm gonna grab it."

"You're crazy," Jason hissed. "That thing's probably rigged." Jason was a bit of a worrier and not much of a risk taker. Well, other than liking the Village People.

"You're such a wuss."

"Pat," I said. "Jason might be right on this one."

"Fine, you sissies. I'll leave it."

Jason and I began walking back to the car when, suddenly, all hell broke loose. We heard a loud splash, then...

"AAAGH!" Pat screamed.

I jerked around, saw Pat holding the dummy, and then noticed that he was dripping wet, covered in some type of black goo. Then it got worse.

WOOP! WOOP! WOOP!

These people had not only set a booby trap but also put an alarm on their dummy.

"Come on," I shouted as I sped towards the car. Jason had beat me and already had the engine started. I dove through the passenger side window and Jason peeled out, leaving a thick dark skid mark down the road. He turned out of the subdivision and headed for the safety of the dirt road across the street.

After going a mile or so, we pulled onto the shoulder and shut off the lights. No one seemed to be following us, so I turned to Jason and we burst into laughter.

We glanced into the empty back seat, and that's when it dawned on us that we had forgotten Pat.

"Oh, crap, Jason! We've got to go back."

"Are you insane," Jason gasped. "There'll be cops all over the place."

There was a brief scary moment of silence, then we burst out laughing again.

After composing ourselves, we decided the safe plan would be to wait a while before going back. In the meantime, we went to another subdivision and busted a few pumpkins thinking maybe someone would see us and call the police, thus drawing them out of the subdivision where Pat was hopefully still hiding.

Thirty minutes later, we reentered enemy territory with our lights off and began the search for our lost comrade. We drove up and down every road twice and no Pat.

"You don't think the cops got him, do you?" Jason asked nervously.

"I hope not," I replied. "But if they did, it would give him something to put on his list of high school accomplishments in the yearbook." Again we laughed.

We turned down another street and suddenly up ahead, we saw a figure rise from the culvert.

"It's gotta be him," I said. And sure enough he came running down the road with the dummy still under his arm. I crawled over into the backseat as he jumped into the car.

"Go! Go!" Pat shouted.

Jason stomped on the gas and we again headed towards the safety of the dirt road across the street. We found the same area of dark shoulder, parked, and shut the car down. That's when the horrible odor hit us.

"What's that smell?" Jason moaned.

"Exactly what you think it is," Pat growled as he opened the door.

Jason and I couldn't help ourselves and burst into convulsive laughter. Apparently the black goo covering Pat contained ammonia, vinegar and feces of some sort. Jason and I could barely get out of the car we were laughing so hard.

"I'm glad you think this is so funny," Pat said as he grabbed a few water balloons from the backseat and splashed them on himself. "Oh, man. I don't think this stuff is coming off."

"Why don't we go to the truck stop down the road," I said as tears rolled down my cheeks from a combination of laughter and stench. "I bet they've got a hose."

"I don't really want him in my car smelling like that," Jason said.

"Tough beans," Pat barked.

"Wait a minute." Jason went to the trunk, grabbed a towel, and laid it on the passenger seat hoping it would serve as a suitable barrier. I jumped behind the wheel, and Jason got in the back seat.

The truck stop was a couple of miles away and I was driving slow, because the deer were thick as molasses out here and you never knew when one would dart out and ruin your day. The road had been clear so far when…

"What's that?" Pat pointed out the windshield to a faint glow in the distance.

"Probably a car." I heard the cooler open. "Jason. What are you doing?"

"It's been a crappy night so far, so I'm gonna nail that car with a water balloon."

"No, you're not," I responded. "You'll cause them to wreck."

"It's a country road. They won't be going fast."

The car was getting closer and Jason was leaning out the window. Suddenly the car was next to us and before I could get the warning out, Jason heaved the balloon, splashing the police cruiser's windshield.

That night, I drove like I had never driven before. The country lane was narrow, so it took a while for the deputy to turn around and pursue us. The lights of the truck stop came into view and I figured if we could get to the parking lot we could hide amongst the trailer trucks. I glanced in the rear-view mirror and in the dusty distance saw that the deputy was now following, blue lights flashing, siren blaring. We had at least a two mile lead on him, and I already pulling into the truck stop parking lot.

I steered the car around back where the overnight drivers parked, and as if it were a sign from above, two trucks were side by side with just enough space for the Camaro to fit in-between. I turned in, slammed on the brakes and shut off the engine. We decided to run inside the diner and act like we'd been there awhile. It was a good plan.

But no. While Jason's car *was* cool and hot, it didn't always run with showroom quality. Sometimes it leaked oil, other times it wouldn't start. But tonight, it decided to have a carburetor problem. The darn thing wouldn't cut off. We were running across the parking lot and the dumb car was coughing, sputtering, and whining. And for some reason, even though I had turned the engine off and had the key in my hand, the radio was still playing. *Macho Man* was blaring through the window, pulsating with each sickening hack of the engine.

I tossed the keys to Jason. "You're on your own."

Pat and I ran to the diner, grabbed a booth, and ducked behind menus. Jason panicked, but managed to crawl under one of the eighteen wheelers just as the deputy pulled into the parking lot. He slowed down and turned on his spotlight scanning everything. Just before he got to where the Camaro was hidden, the car shut down and the Village People left the building. He passed by the car and after circling one more time, the deputy gave up and headed for the interstate on ramp.

We let out sighs of relief, thinking we had gotten away, and could now enjoy a drink and a burger. Then we noticed that everyone had moved away from us. Pat was still stinky. The manager very politely asked us to leave and told us where the hose was.

We had many other Halloween adventures rolling teachers' houses. Rolling a girl's house and getting caught by the police, only to have them help us roll the yard. Stealing a ghost that hung in the Sheriff's yard. We actually got a mention in the paper for that one. The Sheriff was quoted as saying, *"I've had that sheet hanging up every Halloween for the past ten years and no one ever bothered it."*

We kept that sheet in the trunk of Jason's car for a year and just to be cool and show how good we were at pranks, the next year we took it back and re-hung it in the same tree. The next day, the Sheriff was in his yard scratching his head at the sight of the ghost when his neighbor wandered over and asked if everything was all right. The Sheriff nodded, but added that he was perplexed over the taking and return of his ghost and wondered if these pranksters were that good or just stupid and lucky. The neighbor, who just happened to be my Grandfather, commented, "*It was probably a little of both and I'll bet I know who did it.*

The phone call from Sheriff Jones wasn't as surprising as the identity of who had ratted us out. I made a mental note that if I ever committed a felony *not* to confide in Granddad. Sheriff Jones laughed it off, but from then on, anytime something disappeared in Franklin, I got the call.

Halloween had been a great time for us guys and I'm proud to say that while we busted some pumpkins and took some decorations, we never really damaged any property or people. Okay, there was that dog we dyed with red food coloring...

* * *

As I pull into my hotel parking lot, I once again have tears in my eyes. Thinking about those memories makes me think even more of Jason and the regret of letting our relationship fade.

When Pat called, he told me that visitation and the funeral had been postponed for at least a day because a water pipe had burst at the funeral home and flooded all the visitation rooms and the sanctuary. He also told me that Sherry called and wanted to talk to me. He gave me her number and we agreed to meet later for dinner. I told him I would pick him up at work around eight.

I park, grab everything on the front seat, and go to my room.

The manilla envelope still lay on the bed and I agonize over whether to open it or not. The *not* wins out, so instead I check e-mails and to send Melanie the news I have about Jason. There are several business e-mails that I forward to my assistant and a couple of jokes from the boys. I send them a hello, tell them about some of my adventures so far, and send a few pictures I took with my cell phone.

An e-mail isn't appropriate for Mignonne because I want to hear her voice. I dial her number, get her voice mail, and tell her simply that I miss her and that I love her. A long message would get me too emotional and I know her message space is limited. At least I had got to hear her voice.

I glance over at the bedside table clock, 1:30, six and a half hours before dinner. I glance at the manilla envelope and decide it's time.

NINE

I'm in the car, the manilla envelope next to me, and have no clue about it's contents, but I am hopeful that it will give me some insight into Jason's life over the last few years. I pull out of the motel parking lot and drive towards the neighborhood where I grew up with Pat Wilson and first met Jason Maler. The past twenty-four hours had been eventful, and I could only imagine what would come next.

How long had it really been since I heard from Jason? We did e-mail occasionally but never really discussed anything relevant to our lives, just holiday greetings, birthday wishes, and occasional updates on people we knew. I had called him three years ago when his mother died, got his machine and left a message, but now that I think about it, I realize he never called back and I never followed through with another call or a card.

The last time I actually saw him and sat and talked with him had to have been at our twenty year reunion, eight years ago. He wasn't at the golf tournament or family picnic, but he did finally show up at the Saturday night get together. About an hour into the evening, I saw him come through the ballroom door, his sometime girlfriend, Sherry, shadowing him just as she did in high school.

* * *

Pat, his second wife, Reyanne, Mignonne and myself were sitting at a table near the dance floor, close to the DJ's table. I clearly remember standing and waving at Jason, but never got his attention. It was an hour later when he finally approached us. He sat briefly and we spoke for a while, but we really didn't talk about anything, just chatted. After a bit he said he needed to go and find Sherry. Before he left I asked if we could get together before I left town and he said he'd call, but I never heard from him.

* * *

I think back further to the ten year reunion and realize he hadn't even come to that and I had made no effort to contact him. And now that I really think about it, Pat hardly ever discusses Jason when we speak to each other.

It is a sad thought, but at what point do you call a friendship over? Maybe Jason had moved on, found new friends, and a new life that didn't include Pat or myself. He felt he needed us back in high school to fit in, but since then, it seemed he had become his own person, found his own identity, and didn't need to belong to our group of people anymore to feel comfortable.

Jason's personality and likes were always a bit different from mine and Pat's, but that's what made our relationship fun. However, summer before our senior year, he had leaned more towards the alternative, new wave direction that clothes, music, and personalities were taking. He began wearing a lot of black clothes, got his left ear pierced, and tossed his disco albums for the music of The Clash, A Flock of Seagulls, and The Sex Pistols. It was at that time, we met Sherry.

* * *

The summer before our senior year, we were hanging out at the Battlewood subdivision pool in Grassland where Nancy Law lived. I hadn't really gotten to know Mignonne yet, and Pat had a thing for Nancy's friend Laura Anderson. She was always over at Nancy's; therefore, so were we. About two weeks into summer, we were hanging at the pool one Thursday when this gorgeous girl walked through the pool gate. She had a gorgeous face, and even though she had on a baggy t-shirt and shorts we could still tell that she had a killer body. She carried her things to a lounge chair near the corner of the fence away from the crowd. Of course, she got our attention and we coolly watched her from behind our mirrored sunglasses. Even though none of us were dating each other, Nancy and Laura still wanted our undivided attention.

"Who's that?" Jason asked with a nod.

"Don't know," Nancy shrugged. "I think she's new to the neighborhood."

At that moment the mystery girl dropped her shorts and peeled off the t-shirt. Now if you asked most seventeen year old boys who their perfect girl would be, this girl would have been it. I don't recall ever seeing a girl our age who was put together like that.

She was tall, probably five-seven, had flowing auburn hair, smooth olive skin, and more curves than a geometry book. Pat dropped his drink and Jason...well, Jason was love struck. He stood and stared like a zombie, then began walking towards her. Completely oblivious to his surroundings, he took five steps and splashed into the pool. Of course, the rest of us fell out laughing but nothing would stop Jason. He swam to the other side, got out and walked right over to her and sat down. He said something to her, she smiled, and that was it. This girl was way out of any of our leagues, but Jason had been drafted.

An hour later, Nancy and Laura asked Pat and me if we wanted to come over and grill out. Nancy's parents were out of town and they thought it would be fun to have a little party. Sounded great to us. They asked us to go to the store and get some steaks and drinks while they went to the house to make a salad and get some potatoes going. Pat and I quickly grabbed our towels and keys, got to the car, then remembered Jason. He was still with mystery girl. They were now sharing a lounge chair, her sitting between his legs with her back to him so he could rub tanning lotion on her shoulders. Pat went to get him while I toweled off. A few minutes later Pat reappeared and said Jason and Sherry would meet us at Nancy's house.

"So, he introduced you?" I asked.

"Yeah. Her name is Sherry Masters, but it was weird. She already knew my name."

"What do you mean?"

"I walked up and she said, 'Hey, Pat.'"

I shrugged. "Jason must have told her."

We drove to the store and arrived at Nancy's about forty-five minutes later with steaks, bread, drinks, and brownies. The girls were on the patio and already had the grill warming. Pat put the steaks on, so I walked over to where Jason and Sherry were playing with Nancy's chocolate lab, Alex.

"Hey, guys," I said.

"Hey, Scott," both responded.

Alex came to me and rolled over for me to rub his stomach. Sherry walked over and squatted beside me while Jason went to help Pat.

"He must know you pretty well," she said.

"Yeah," I said while scratching Alex. "Alex and I have been doing this for a few years."

She laughed then leaned in close to scratch along. The gentle breeze blew her hair across my face and the scent was incredible, a perfect blend of shampoo, perfume, and sun tan lotion. She smelled like...summer.

"Have you got a dog, Scott?"

"Yeah," I nodded. "A miniature dachshund, Hot Dog."

"Really? I would have pictured you with a big dog like Alex here."

"Well, Hot Dog's three feet long and weighs forty two pounds, sort of a big, low profile kind of dog."

She raised her lavender eyes to mine. "That's cute, Scott."

We stood. "I'm sorry, Sherry, is it? Do we know each other?"

She smiled. "We know of each other, yes."

"How so?"

"You're going to have to figure that out." With that, she walked back towards the house and joined Jason on the patio.

Sherry and Jason spent the rest of summer together as a couple. You very seldom saw one without the other, and that was cool. I had never seen Jason so happy. He was truly in love for the first time, and she seemed completely in love and devoted to him also. When they weren't together and just us guys went to play golf or to see a movie, there was always a little love note or flower on Jason's windshield when we got to the car. She was a sweet, romantic, intelligent, beautiful girl who remained maddeningly mysterious throughout the entire summer.

Fast forward a few weeks later, the first day of school, and I was cruising the halls, saying hey to all the teachers and seeing if anyone new and cute had transferred to Franklin High School this year. As I slid down the rail of the handicapped ramp, I heard my name.

"Hey, Scott."

I glanced back up the ramp thinking the voice had come from behind, then I felt the tap on my shoulder.

"Hey."

I turned around and looked right into the sunglasses of Star, a popular member of the Goth group of kids we referred to as vampires. They are the ones who wear white make-up and black eye shadow, have raven hair, and dress entirely in black clothes.

I got to know her fairly well last year when she was a sophomore and we were both on the student council. The vampires had decided they needed class representation so they pushed Star into it. I had been told by the student council sponsor that she was very smart, rumor was a 4.0 GPA. She was very nice and really got involved with the program. Most of us agreed that Star was different than the rest of the vampires. She just seemed a bit more…(I don't want to say normal because in high school who or what is exactly normal) but more toned down, or conservative than the others.

"Hi, Star," I said casually. "How was your summer?"

"You should know," she shrugged "I spent most of it with you."

All right, I knew a lot of people in high school and had never limited myself in friendships. I hung out with jocks, socks, geeks, freaks, preps, brains, pains, blacks, whites, yellows, reds, and sometimes, even a vampire or two. Hey, you never know what type of situation life is going to bring, so it's good to be connected to all types of people. Over the summer, we had gone to many places, seen a bunch of people, and attended quite a few good parties, but I had absolutely no recollection of ever hanging out with Star or even seeing her for that matter.

The hall was getting crowded so Star took my hand and pulled me closer to her locker.

"Star…?"

She removed her sunglasses, raised her face to mine and our eyes locked. Those beautiful lavender eyes.

* * *

I remember that day like it was yesterday.

My cell phone vibrates and hoping it might be Mignonne, I pull onto the shoulder of the road so I can talk safely. I don't recognize the number on the screen.

"Scott Sawyer," I answer.

"Hey, Scott."

I didn't know the number but I definitely know the voice.

"Hey, Sherry. I was just thinking about you."

TEN

It's been seven years since I've seen Sherry Masters, and at least four since I've heard anything about her. Pat said that she and Jason had a falling out and that Jason hardly spoke to her. I had questioned Pat further but to no avail.

"Sometimes relationships just run their course," was all he said.

A true statement, but this was Jason and Sherry. They had been together, either as lovers or at the least close friends for almost twenty-three years.

I called Jason shortly after my discussion with Pat and left a message for him to call. At the same time, I sent Sherry a card that said I was thinking about her and if she needed to talk to someone, please call. I never heard a thing from either of them.

These thoughts crossed my mind as she spoke.

"Did Pat tell you that I wanted to talk you?" There's an accusatory tone in her voice. Nothing new. She never really seemed to like Pat that much, didn't think he was trustworthy. Probably because Pat always flirted with her.

"He did tell me." I didn't want to get Pat into trouble by lying, but I really didn't want her mad at me either. "But I just got the message a little while ago and haven't had a chance to call."

"Oh. Okay." There's a brief moment of silence. I guess she's trying to decide how to proceed. "I was wondering...I was wondering if you had seen Jason's friend, Lucinda, yet?"

Was there a bit of a tone when she said *Lucinda?* "Yes, actually. I ran into her this morning..."

She interrupts, "So do you have the letter?"

"I do."

Her voice calms. "And...?"

"I haven't read it yet, Sherry."

"Why not?"

I think about telling her I was just on my way to the special place where Jason wanted me to read it but decide not to. "I haven't found the proper time yet."

It's so quiet on the other end of the line that, for a moment, I think she's hung up on me. Then I hear her breathing.

"Scott...I think you should come by and see me before you read it."

"Okay. When?"

"I'm home now."

She gives me directions and I head for her house. She now lived in Spring Hill, a town about fifteen miles south of Franklin near the Maury County line. As a teenager and into my early twenties, Spring Hill was a tiny community with one flashing light, but then General Motors opened the Saturn plant there and the place boomed. Columbia Highway, the highway connecting Franklin and Spring Hill, was now thickly bordered with strip malls, fast food restaurants, schools, and subdivisions.

Sherry's directions are pretty good but I still manage to get lost. Too many street signs and turns. I really miss the simplicity of Oahu where only one road circles the entire island. I stop to get my bearings and realize I turned right when I should have turned left. Seven minutes later, I turn into Sherry's subdivision, pass through two stop signs, and know without a doubt I've found Sherry's house.

Her 1974 silver Volkswagen from high school sits in her driveway. I know it's the same one because the Merit cigarette company logo is still painted on the side.

Back in late seventies and early eighties, you could smoke at school. There was a yellow line painted thirty feet from the back of the building and smoking was permitted as long as you stayed behind that line. The smokers were a click just like the other social groups and were proud to have their little spot. And every year, one or two of the cigarette companies would pick someone on the smoking line and offer them a free paint job at the end of the school year if they could paint the company logo on the side of the car.

Sherry, or at that time, Star, had allowed them to have her Volkswagen Beetle for two years and I guess she never had it repainted. I wonder why?

As I pull into her driveway, I see her standing in the front window and wave. She waves back and opens the front door.

"Hey, Sherry," I say as I get out of the car and walk to the door. She doesn't return my hello, just bites her lip, wraps her arms around my neck, and breaks down. We stand in the doorway for at least ten minutes, not speaking, just holding each other.

Funny the things you notice at a time like this. Her head rests on my chest just beneath my face. I glance down and happy to see her long hair isn't colored vampire black anymore. Instead, it's the beautiful chestnut color I remember from that summer so long ago, and it smells wonderful.

She finally raises her face and those stunning lavender eyes meet mine.

"Hey," she says with a sniffle, then pulls free and runs her hands through her hair. "I must look a mess. Sorry."

She's barefoot, not wearing any make-up and is dressed in faded jeans and a t-shirt, both showing she hasn't lost her figure.

"Sherry, I don't think I've ever seen you look more beautiful."

She gives me a slightly crooked smile. "You always did say the right thing at the right time."

I'm not sure whether to be insulted or not but it doesn't matter. She takes my hand and leads me through her small and simply decorated house to the deck. Her backyard is nicely landscaped with a multitude of flower beds, and has an in-ground pool and hot tub.

"Can I get you something to eat, drink?" she asks.

"No thanks, Sherry. I'm good."

We sit in lounge chairs near the bubbling spa tub.

"You are good, Scott," she shrugs. "You've always been a good guy."

"You're sweet."

"I mean it," she says with a nod. "Back in high school, you were always so nice to everybody no matter who they were or what they looked like. You weren't ever one of those guys who tried to take advantage of anyone. People could count on you to do the right thing."

Where's this going? I wonder.

"And now you sponsor all sorts of charities and make donations to schools."

"Just trying to give a little back." I decide to change the subject. The stereo is on and playing a song I recognize. "Would that be some smooth jazz I'm hearing?"

She smiles. "Yes. A band called *Everything but the Girl*."

"That's funny," I laugh. "Quite a few years ago, I remember listening to this very CD and someone, who was dressed in black and had just pierced her..."

"Don't go there."

"Sorry," I say. "Anyway, she was dressed in black, wore dark blue eye shadow, very attractive by the way, and she asked me why I spent my money on crappy music like *this*."

She cuts her eyes at me. "And *your* response was that someday, I might appreciate the coolness of jazz."

"Exactly."

We laugh, then her eyes fill with tears.

"I know what you're doing, Scott, and I appreciate it. But I can't and won't be distracted."

"Sorry."

Sherry turns sideways, faces me, and lights a cigarette. I notice the dark circles around her eyes and the sag in her shoulders. Even though she looks wonderful, I can't help but notice that she looks very tired and a bit old, and I wonder if it's from her wild life as a Goth in her youth, or if it has to do with something much deeper.

"I wanted to talk to you about Jason before you read his letter. There are things…" She closes her eyes tightly, trying to fight the emotions that are welling up inside of her.

I reach out and take the cigarette from her trembling fingers.

"Come here." I take her hand and pull her over to my lounge chair that's built for two. She sits on my knees, then curls up in my lap. I stroke her hair and tell her to take her time.

She takes a few deep breaths and begins. "Four years ago Jason was getting in shape to run a marathon."

"Jason Maler?"

"I know," she sniffs. "Doesn't sound like the Jason you knew, but he had really changed. He quit smoking and drinking, ate healthy, worked out, and started running."

"Really."

"Yeah." She looks up and I notice the wrinkles at the corners of her mouth from years of smoking and possibly frowns. "It was after I had my first miscarriage."

"I'm so sorry, Sherry. I didn't know."

She lays her head back down against my chest.

"No one did. We decided not to tell anyone until we were sure. Back then the ages of thirty-seven and thirty-eight were considered too old to be having a baby…"

"Wait a minute," I interrupt. "You were thirty-seven, so Jason was thirty-eight?"

She nods.

"So, were you guys pregnant at the twenty year reunion? Is that why Jason was being so distant and why we didn't even get to talk to you?"

Her body shakes with sobs. "There's so much you don't know." She sits up, turns around to face me, and crosses her legs. "He was mad at me that night."

I shake my head, not understanding. "Why would he be mad at you?"

She brushes away the tears. "It's no secret I was wild in high school. If I hadn't met you guys I probably would've ended up dead from drugs or alcohol long ago. You all were popular and successful and included me in your group of friends. That was important to me, so I didn't want to screw it up. Then, you know, when you and Pat went off to college, Jason and I, were kind of lost. So, we just hung out, went to school part time, and worked. He watched over me and protected me." She suddenly sits up straight and pulls her long hair back into a ponytail and wraps a rubber band from her wrist around it. "But whenever you guys came back into town, you always made time for us, acted like we were still part of the group." She pulls out another cigarette.

"Sherry," I say. "You don't have to tell me all of this."

She shakes her head and puts the cigarette back. "You need to know. It will explain a lot."

"Okay."

"A couple of years later, you and Mignonne got really serious and Pat married that Sasha chick. And all of a sudden Jason felt like he didn't belong, didn't have his stability anymore."

I feel the tears coming and close my eyes.

"No, Scott. I'm not saying this to make you feel bad. It's just…you know how he was. He needed to belong to something and you guys had moved on, grown up. And by that time I had dropped out of community college and started going to graphic design school. That crowd was more my type of people, you know, introverted, artsy. Several of my *vampire* friends from high school were there and it wasn't long before I fell into the old routine and started using again. Pot. Cocaine. Tequila."

"And Jason?"

"Jason," she pauses. "He started drinking a lot and using too. He said if I was going to kill myself then he was too, because he didn't want to live without me."

That sounds just like him, I think, so co-dependent and desperate to be loved. I knew he was drinking heavily but didn't know about the drugs.

"Well," she continues. "That made me sober up fast. Jason was the only person who ever loved me enough to say he would die for me. So we both quit, then he got depressed. I told him he should call you or Pat and tell you guys he needed help. But he was mad at Pat."

"Why?" I ask.

"Remember the New Year's Eve that you and Mignonne didn't go to Pat's house."

"Sure. It was 1989. The New Year's Eve before we got married."

"Right. Well, turns out, that's the day Pat's first wife, Sasha, told him she wanted a divorce, so he was already hammered by the time we got to the party. As usual, Jason and I were in some stupid fight and I started looking for Pat to see if he could talk to Jason. I found him on the back porch, then fell into his arms crying with my problems. I had no clue of what had happened to Pat earlier in the day, and didn't realize he was drunk until he lifted my face to his and said, *"I've always been in love with you, Sherry."* Then, he kissed me and…well…I kissed him back.

We were pressed against the wall of the house rubbing against each other when Jason came outside and saw us. They took a couple of swings at each other before Pat fell off the porch and Jason took me home."

This was new. "Did he and Jason ever talk about it?"

"Never. And Jason never really seemed to forgive him, or me for that matter. So neither of them ever said anything to you?" She asks.

"No." The next time we were all together was a year later for all of the events leading up to mine and Mignonne's wedding. This finally explained why Pat and Jason seemed so distant from each other at all of the parties and even in the wedding pictures. How could I have not realized? It also explained why Pat didn't ever talk much about Jason anymore, and why he had drank so much the first night I was here. He was feeling ashamed and guilty.

"So that's why he didn't come to the ten year reunion?" I ask.

"Jason was really drinking heavily during that time, and he was so ashamed. He also was afraid that he might hit Pat or do something stupid at the reunion."

"And the twenty?"

"Oh, God," she gasps. "That was the best and worst time of my life."

"What happened?"

"The good part…I was working at Graphix International as an artist and was doing really well. I was sober and healthy and Jason and I had started talking about getting married. And...he had started painting. I never knew he was so talented as an artist. Did you?"

"Not really. He always drew cars and album covers but nothing really hang-on-the-wall artsy. I did notice a painting in Lucinda's office. It was signed, J.M."

"Yeah, the flamingoes. That was his." She nods and seems to go somewhere else in her mind.

"And what was the bad time, Sherry?"

She focuses again. "Jason was becoming a different person...not in a bad way. He started doing some construction, said he wanted to make things with his hands, use his artistic side to create. It really pissed me off."

"Why?"

"I just figured it was another excuse to goof off and not make any kind of money or...commitment."

"Commitment?"

"To me, Scott. I wanted to take the next step, get married, and if he wasn't going to buckle down and get a real job then we couldn't ever afford to have a family."

"What happened."

"I broke things off with him and left for a graphic design conference in Chicago. He called and called but I wouldn't answer." She looks away, then turns back. "I felt really good for about sixteen hours, then the bottom fell out. I went to the bar and started drinking. A...friend of mine showed up there and well he...was very comforting."

"I'm sorry," is all I can say.

"I wasn't," she says harshly. "I had been with Jason since I was sixteen years old, and I truly believed it was good for me to be with someone else so I could realize how good I had it with Jason."

I've heard this kind of logic many times before and it never turns out well. "I assume he found out."

"I wasn't going to tell him. Anyway, when I got home from Chicago, I started feeling guilty, told him, apologized and begged him to forgive me." She twists her fingers.

"Sherry, we can stop."

"Three weeks later I found out I was pregnant."

I don't blink, move, or even breathe. I don't want her to think I'm judging her.

"So I got a friend to take me to the clinic and I had an abortion. Jason sensed something was wrong and a couple of days later I finally broke down and told him."

"What was his reaction?"

"He was upset, naturally, but not so much about the affair as he was the abortion. He asked if I had told the father."

"And had you?"

"No. But I decided Jason was right and I called him." She uncrosses her legs, stands up, and stretches. She then turns back towards me. "Turns out…this guy had found out he was infertile a couple of years before. He couldn't have kids."

I quickly stand and move towards her. She puts out her hand and stops me.

"It was Jason's baby, Scott." She runs inside, goes into the bathroom, and slams the door shut.

I walk over to the deck rail and start to cry. I cry for Sherry, for Jason, for the baby, for this whole mess that has affected so many lives. When the sobbing subsides, I drop to my knees and thank God for Mignonne and Clay and Cameron and for the wonderful life we share, and I ask Him to give me the strength to get through what lies ahead.

ELEVEN

I'm back in the car now, heading towards Pat's office to take him to dinner.

Sherry had locked herself in the bathroom for thirty minutes, and when I knocked she told me to go. I pleaded with her to come out and talk some more but she was spent, emotionally exhausted. When I asked if we could continue later, she said she would meet me for breakfast tomorrow at Sonya's breakfast cafe near the movie theater at nine a.m.

There are so many questions, but I understand her need to tell me things when she's comfortable.

I pull into the parking lot and see Pat sitting on the hood of his car. He hops off and gets in.

"What's up?" he asks casually.

I really don't know. "I just came from Sherry's house."

Pat's eyes quickly drop. "What did she have to say?"

"Lots of things." I shake my head in frustration. "Pat, why didn't you tell me any of this?"

"Any of what?"

"Don't do that. You know exactly what. The fight between you and Jason. Jason's drinking and drug use. The baby?"

Pat takes a deep breath. "I don't know what to say. Those were rough times for me, Jason, and Sherry. My marriage was falling apart. Jason and Sherry fought all of the time and she always came to me for comfort. I was pretty drunk that New Year's Eve and when she fell into my arms…"

"She was Jason's girl, Pat"

"And she's a beautiful woman, Scott," he shouts. "I've had a thing for her since we met her at the pool all those years ago." His face turns red, and I can't tell if it's from anger or embarrassment.

"Pat…"

"Don't judge me, Scott. You weren't here. You weren't here when he was blind stinking drunk or stoned out of his mind. You weren't here to bail his butt out of jail when he got in fights. You weren't here to see how he took Sherry for granted, how he didn't appreciate her." A tear trickles down his left cheek. "You weren't here…when…"

"I'm sorry, Pat."

"Forget it, man." He gets out of the car and slams the door.

I get out and try to catch up to him, but he gets in his car and speeds away.

"What a mess," I say to myself.

Not sure what to do now, I try to call the one person I can always count on. The person who loves and cares for me unconditionally, but again I have no luck.

"Hi. This is Mignonne Sawyer. Sorry I missed your call, but I am unable to answer right now. Please leave a message and I will get back to you as soon as possible."

"Hey, Sweetie. It's me. Just wanted to hear your voice. I love you and miss you. Bye." Where could she be?

I climb back into the car and glance at the dashboard clock, 7:45. I flip open my phone again and dial another number. She answers. Fifteen minutes later, I arrive at Jackson's Cafe where

Nancy Law and Laura Anderson are waiting in the parking lot, sitting in Laura's Volvo convertible.

I pull in beside them. "Hey, girls," I say through the driver's side window. "Thanks for coming."

"Glad to," Nancy says from the passenger side.

I get out of the car and begin to open her door when she stops me.

"Aren't we going in?" I ask.

"No," says Laura from the driver's seat. "We've got another plan."

About that time Ms. Mona walks out of the café with a brown paper bag. "Hello, Scott."

"Hey, Ms. Mona."

She hands the bag through the window to Nancy. "Thanks, Mona."

"You're welcome, dear. You all enjoy." She then pats my cheek and goes back inside the restaurant.

Laura starts the car, "Get in, Scott."

I climb into the backseat behind Nancy and off we go. Nancy opens the bag and the scintillating smell of fried chicken, mashed potatoes, and biscuits wafts through the car.

"Hey, Nancy. What do I owe you for the food?"

She turns around. "Not a thing." She then hands me a plastic to go box. "Ms. Mona's compliments."

I pry the top off and smile because Ms. Mona has remembered my love for her heavenly banana pudding. I recap the box and place it on the seat next to me.

Glancing up I see Nancy is turned sideways in her seat.

"Tough day, honey?" she says with a gentle smile.

"Yeah," Laura adds. "You sounded pretty down when you called."

"You could say that."

Laura tucks a stray strand of blond hair behind her ear. "Want to talk about it?"

I glance out the side window as Laura turns off the road onto a paved lane I know well.

"It started okay, but then…" I give them a play by play of the day, from eating breakfast at Clarence's to my brief, heated, conversation with Pat. Neither one of them says anything, just listen as I talk. Ten minutes later, Laura stops the car and we get out.

I walk a few steps and stop at the edge of the overlook.

"Wow. The view has really changed." We always called the road Dead Man's Hill, but Long Lane is the proper name. It's a steep graded lane off of Franklin Road, about five miles outside of Franklin and two miles from the city Brentwood. The Dead Man nickname had been given when a twenty-year old guy had scaled the hill after a big snow and sledded from the top. When he reached the bottom he was going so fast he couldn't stop and slid right into the main road and was hit by a car. A *No Sledding or Bicycling* sign had been put up shortly afterwards.

It was the highest point in Williamson County and in high school had been a favorite spot for teens to come and hang out, or make out depending on the crowd. The hill was so steep many older cars couldn't make the trip, and others could only do so if the passengers got out and walked and you turned off the air conditioner or heater. During high school no developer had had any luck building on the hill because the machines couldn't function on the steep grade, but it seemed someone had finally been successful because there were now several mansions gracing the lower part of the hillside. Huge homes with in-ground pools and plenty of landscaping and mood lighting. There was a cul-de-sac at the top of the hill now and some of the trees had been cleared away so the view of Franklin and Brentwood was spectacular. There had been nowhere near the number of homes or lights viewable from here all those years ago, and there was now a vast, haunting glow towards the east. I guess Nancy notices me staring in that direction.

"The mall," she explains sadly. "Kind of takes away the romance of the night skyline." She takes my hand and leads me back to the blanket where Laura has set up the food.

I cross my legs and sit down with a groan so common to my body these days.

"This is nice, girls. Thanks."

We eat Ms. Mona's incredible food in silence for a while, then I speak.

"I guess I've really upset Pat."

"Pat will be okay, Scott," Laura says. "All of this is hitting him pretty hard."

Nancy lets out a quiet sob, and Laura places her hand on Nancy's shoulder.

"It's hitting all of us pretty hard, and the best thing we can do is be here for each other."

"Nancy?" I ask. "Would you be willing to tell me more about you and Jason?"

She puts down her glass of wine, wipes her eyes with a napkin, and brings her knees up under her chin. "Laura always tries to keep me updated on everything and everybody back home, so I knew that Jason was single again, and had had some problems with drinking and drugs. That night, when Laura and I ran into him at the restaurant, he joined us for dinner and just started talking. He told us everything that had been going on in his life and also apologized for anytime he may have said anything bad to me or taken me for granted as a friend. Then he told me that he had had a bit of a crush on me in high school, before he met

Sherry, and had always wondered what dating me would have been like."

She starts crying again and I offer her my handkerchief.

She and Laura both laugh.

"Still carrying these?" Nancy says through tears.

"You bet," I answer. Over the years, many of my handkerchiefs had been ruined by mascara or eye shadow. "You never know when a pretty girl might need one."

Nancy wipes her eyes, then continues. "Laura left early that night, and Jason said he would take me over to Laura's later on. We hung for hours, just talking and walking around town. After a while he asked if he could hold my hand, and, of course I said yes. Then later, when he dropped me off at Laura's, he kissed me and it was wonderful." With that, she stops and starts eating a piece of chicken.

I decide not to press her any further. "Laura, can you tell me anything about Jason?"

"Such as?"

"Let's start with his art and carpentry."

Nancy stands with her glass of wine. "Excuse me." She walks away towards the overlook.

I start to go with her, but Laura gently touches my arm. "Let her be."

I settle back down and Laura begins.

"Jason was always talented, Scott, always scribbling some stupid picture on his desk or on one of his books."

"I remember, but they were just silly cars, album covers, cartoons and stuff like that. I don't remember anything that really looked like art."

Her eyes tear up but I don't have another hanky so I hand her a napkin. "He kept a lot of that stuff hidden away from us," she sniffs.

"Why?"

She shrugs. "I believe he was afraid of what we might think. You know how he really didn't fit in with us until you guys took him under your wing. I believe when he started hanging with Sherry, some of his earlier personality and interests resurfaced, and he felt we might not accept that or think that he was silly."

I shake my head, unbelieving. "Do you know that for sure or are you just speculating?"

"Sherry told me that. She's an incredible artist herself and she helped him develop his style and made him unafraid to express himself. After you and Pat left for college, he just sort of threw himself into being creative, and he was great at it. The houses he remodeled. The paintings he did. It was amazing. For the first time in a long time, he was happy and he was making good money."

"I wish I would have known how unhappy he was before," I whisper.

"He didn't want to burden anyone with his problems. He needed to find his own happiness."

"He burdened Sherry?"

Laura's eyes shift downward. "Not with everything."

There it is. "What are you and everyone else not telling me, Laura?"

The answer comes from behind. "He had cancer, Scott." Nancy walks over and rejoins us on the blanket.

"Wh…what?" The anger grows in my mind. The sadness wells in my heart. "And nobody told me?"

Nancy wraps her arm around me. "None of us knew, Scott."

"How could that be?"

"We found out the night he died." Laura reaches over and takes a long pull on the wine bottle. "I was with Sherry when the police called about Jason's crash. I went with her to the hospital and while we were waiting in the emergency room the doctor came in and told us three things." She pauses.

"What?"

"First, he told us Jason was dead. He had been killed on impact. When the Camaro hit the embankment, Jason's head slammed into the steering wheel, crushed the temporal lobe of his skull and caused severe a bleed-out. Second, he told us about the cancer and how he had kept it a secret as a promise to Jason. He was diagnosed about five years ago…"

"Scott?" Nancy takes the wine bottle from Laura and drinks. "Did you know about the abortion?"

"I just found that out from Sherry."

"Wait," Laura continues. "A few years before that, Sherry got pregnant with Jason's child. The two of them were very excited and understandably sort of scared. They started talking about getting married, and having a big wedding and party at Jason's parent's old farm. Sherry was thrilled. All she could talk about was how much she loved Jason and how this child was going to make everything between them okay. Anyway, at six weeks she started having problems, and a few days later she miscarried."

"Jeez," I mutter.

"Everything checked out okay and the doctor told them they could try again in a couple of months. About seven months later they got pregnant again…and six weeks later she miscarried again." Laura reaches for the wine again. "Jason freaked. He just knew it was from all of the alcohol and drugs they had used before." She takes a sip. "But all of Sherry's tests came back fine, so he figured it must be him and he went on a total health binge, healthy diet, vitamins, exercise, the whole shebang. He started jogging, working out with weights. He became obsessed and he looked great and said he felt better."

"He did," Nancy adds.

"Then suddenly he starts having problems with his back, figures he's pulled a muscle or something and lets it slide. After a week with no exercise, his pain started getting worse and Sherry convinced him to go to the doctor. Regular x-rays and blood tests were inconclusive so he had an M.R.I..." She pauses.

I move away from Nancy and stand, feeling weak as the blood rushes back into my legs.

"Where was it?" I ask.

"In his spine," Nancy answers. "A large mass where the neck joins the spine."

I glance up at the full moon. "And no one contacted me."

Laura stands and walks over to me. "He didn't tell Sherry or anyone, Scott," she says again. "In fact, after the M.R.I. is when he broke up with Sherry, just cut her out of his life."

"I can't believe that."

Laura takes my hand. "I like to think he did it for a good reason."

"Such as?"

"Such as...he wanted to protect her from the pain and suffering he would experience. He wanted her to move on and forget him."

"So he died with her angry at him?"

"No," Laura explains. "A few months ago he called her and said he wanted to talk. She met him at the farm...where he begged her forgiveness and told her she was the best thing that ever happened to him." She lets go of my hand and puts her arm around my waist. "Scott, he told her that he loved her more than anything or anyone and hoped that one day she would understand his reason for letting her go." She squeezes me tightly. "Then later on..."

"She got pregnant again," I finish Laura's statement.

Laura nods. "And she had an abortion thinking it was someone else's."

"And it was really Jason's," Nancy says as she joins us.

"What about you, Nancy? You didn't know anything about the cancer?"

"Not until after he died. Laura told me about the night at the hospital," she whispers. "But I knew something was wrong a while back when he called me out of the blue and said that he didn't think he was right for me and I deserved better. I got angry, figuring he had found someone else, so I broke things off, then met my husband. You know how that turned out. After my divorce, Laura told me Jason was still available and I really hoped when I came home this week I could find him and see if we could work things out. But..." She begins crying again.

I put my other arm around Nancy.

"Laura? You said the doctor told you and Sherry three things. What was the third?"

She raises her head from my shoulder. "He told us about the note they had found in Jason's pocket. The one with your name on it."

I pull both girls close to me. "Dear, God. How did we all grow so far apart?"

TWELVE

A couple of hours later, Nancy and Laura drop me off at my car. We spent most of the night just holding each other and crying, hoping our time together would offer some healing. A pact was made between the three of us to never let our friendship grow this far apart again and I sincerely hope we meant it.

They ask me to join them for breakfast a little later, but I tell them I have something important attend to and I'll see them later in the day, probably at visitation. I kiss each of them on the cheek, thank them for the evening, and get out.

It's three a.m., Clarence's Cafe is closed and my car is the only one in the parking lot. The air is still and the night is quiet, almost too quiet. Leaning against the car, I flip open my cell phone, hoping I will have a message from Mignonne, but there isn't one. It's only eleven-o'clock in Hawaii, so I try her again and still get the voice mail. Where could she be? And why hadn't she returned any of my calls in the past few hours?

"I really miss you and wish I could hear your voice. So much has happened. It just feels…" I stop, knowing this is a conversation for another time. "I love you. Please call me soon."

I hang up, close my eyes, and take a deep breath. A gentle breeze stirs and the smell of lilac wafts through the car window, reminding me of so many late spring evenings. I take a deeper breath and detect another scent mingling with the lilac, a familiar scent of cologne.

"Hey, Pat," I say without turning around. Getting no response, I turn and see him leaning against the trunk of my car. I decide not to say anything, just see what happens.

"I owe you…" He stops and clears his throat a couple of times but doesn't seem to be able to get beyond that phrase. There are tears on his face. "I owe you…an apology and an explanation."

"You don't…"

He holds up his hand. "Let me talk, okay."

"Okay."

"You're my best friend, Scott. Even though we're several thousand miles apart you've always been there when I needed you." He walks around to the hood and hops on it. "I, on the other hand, have been a terrible friend." He shakes his head as if denying something. "When you married Mignonne and moved to Hawaii, I was so…envious. You had it all, a great wife, huge success. You were living the dream and I was stuck here, mired in an awful marriage to a girl I never really loved, stuck in a dead-end job."

I remain silent, knowing he's not finished.

"Then," Pat continues, "after my second marriage failed, I decided to get my life together. I bought the house, opened my business, and started looking for the *right* girl." He smiles. "You know what's funny? I always knew who the right girl was…" He stops and raises his eyes to mine. "My second best friend's girlfriend."

"Sherry," I say.

"Yeah," He nods, then glances back at the asphalt. "You ever felt the pain of being in love with someone when she belongs to someone else, especially a good friend?"

I feel it's a rhetorical question and remain quiet.

"There were times, Scott. Times when Sherry and Jason were fighting and she would come to me just to have a friend to talk to. She would cry on my shoulder and say things like, 'Why couldn't I have hooked up with you, Pat?' 'I love you, Pat.' 'Say you'll always be here for me, Pat.'" He wipes a tear from his cheek. "I just couldn't take it anymore…and I finally told her how I felt."

"New Year's Eve, 1989."

He looks at me again. "Did Jason tell you?"

'No. Sherry did when I met with her yesterday."

"What else did she tell you?"

"Well," I say. "She told me about you and Jason having a falling out…and…the miscarriages. Then she told me about the affair with a friend… And the abortion."

He winces, as if I'm about to hit him. "So you know then."

It's more of a statement than a question.

"Yeah. I know she thought it was someone else's baby and later found out it was Jason's."

He eyes close. "And?"

I'm confused. "And what?"

"I was the friend, Scott." He hops off of the hood and sits on the sidewalk. "We were both in Chicago. I was there for a Cub's game. She was attending a graphic design conference. I knew she was there, but we hadn't planned on getting together or anything. The game ended early, so I decided to run by her hotel and…"

"What?"

"I found her in the bar, drunk out of her mind. I helped her to her room and she asked me to stay."

"Pat…"

He explains. "I didn't take advantage of her. But she just kept on kissing me and telling me she wanted me. I tried my best, but then…"

I walk over and sit beside him.

"She said she loved me and wanted us to be together. She was tired of Jason and his moodiness, tired of being taken for granted." He shakes his head again. "It was too much for me to resist."

"How did you react when she called about the baby?"

"Shocked, and upset."

"Upset?"

"I was tested during my first marriage. I can't have kids…never really found out why. But since neither of my two wives got pregnant, it must be true."

"I'm sorry, Pat."

"No, I'm the one that's sorry. I should have told you all of this a long time ago."

"Pat?"

"Yeah?"

"Have you talked to Sherry?"

He nods. "Every once in a while."

"I mean, have you talked to her about…well…you two getting together and trying to find those feelings again…as a couple."

He scoffs. "I appreciate your romance and optimism, Scott. But I don't think that could ever happen. Too much water under the bridge." He stands. "Are we cool?"

"Sure," I answer with a handshake. "We're always cool."

"Good," he replies, then pulls me up and hugs me. "I couldn't stand losing another friend."

"Never."

He lets go and backs away. "You want to give me a ride home?"

We get in the car and head towards his house. He tells me that the funeral home called and everything's working again so visitation had been rescheduled for one-o'clock, followed by the funeral at three-o'clock.

The dashboard clock reads four a.m. as I pull into his driveway.

"You want to hook up later on?" he asks as he gets out of the car.

"Can't. I got something to do."

"Need me to go with you?"

"No thanks."

"Okay. I'll see you."

I wait till he's inside, then back out of his driveway. What a night it's been.

A light rain begins to fall, so I turn on the wipers and hope that the weather won't be bad for Jason's funeral. I drive slowly, listening to the rain against my windshield, and say a silent prayer.

"Amen," I whisper to myself as I pull into the motel parking lot.

Because of the late hour, there's hardly any traffic and every stop light is green all the way to my motel. The rain is falling heavier now, so I dash to my room, scan my card key, and push the door open. Without turning on the room light, I make my way to the bathroom, click on the bathroom light, and begin unbuttoning my wet shirt.

"Before you go any further, I think you should know that you're not alone."

I jump and spin around.

Sherry Masters clicks on the bedside lamp. "Hey," she says. She's sitting on the bed with her long legs crossed.

"Hey. What are you doing here? I thought we were going to meet for breakfast."

She takes a strand of her long auburn hair and nervously begins twisting it with her right index finger. As I watch, I understand why Jason and Pat fell for her. She's a beautiful and smart woman who exudes an innocence and a need to be taken care of.

"I didn't want to wait 'till breakfast," she explains. "After you left my house, I sat in the bathroom for several hours and thought about everything. Thought about all of it until my brain was exhausted and I just couldn't think anymore."

I'm not quite ready for this yet, so I change the subject for a second. "Sherry. How did you get into my room?"

"The desk clerk is my cousin," she replies matter-of-factly.

"Oh." I cross the room and grab a dry t-shirt from my suitcase. Then I get comfortable in one of the room's wingback chairs, figuring this is probably going to take a while.

She begins. "Scott, Jason was a wonderful person, and my life would not have been the same if I hadn't met him and fallen in love with him. But I hadn't been in love with him for quite some time, and I'm positive he wasn't in love with me anymore." She sighs. "Don't get me wrong. We still loved each other, but I think we outgrew each other a long time ago, and were too frightened to move on because we had been together for so long." She raises her eyes to mine as if she expects a comment but I sit perfectly still and don't make a sound. "Scott, Jason was sick."

"I know."

"How?"

"Nancy Law and Laura Anderson told me."

She nods. "I had no idea until he died, and I wonder how he could have been so sick and not tell me, or anyone for that matter. I felt angry, hurt, and betrayed. Then, I understood why he broke up with me. He didn't want me to suffer with him. He wanted me to move forward with my life."

I move to the bed and sit beside her. "Jason was different, Sherry. We all knew that, but this story sounds very familiar."

"How so?" she asks.

"Jason's mom died of ovarian cancer when he was fourteen. Jason didn't know she had cancer until three weeks before she died and he found out then because he overheard his mom and dad talking."

"But he was a child. That's different."

"Not to him. To him it was a way to spend as much time as possible with his mom without always being sad." I pause to gather my thoughts. She senses it and takes my hand. "To him, he was protecting you from being sad, giving you time to get over him before he died."

She begins to cry. "I guess I should be grateful to him."

"No, you should be mad as hell at him," I shout. "It's not fair to spend your entire life with someone and not be able to be there for them when they're dying."

Sherry squeezes my hand and in a calm voice says, "Are you talking about me…or you, Scott?"

With that, the tears come and I slump over. "Sherry, I completely failed him as a friend."

She rubs my back and lays her head on my shoulder. "No, Scott. You didn't. He loved you…Scott, sit up and look at me."

I obey and her eyes are fixed on mine.

"He loved you more than anyone else. You were not only his friend. You were more like a brother. And even though you guys hadn't spoken to one another or been together for a long time, he never stopped loving you. That's why when he died, he left…"

"The note with my name on it." I sigh.

"Exactly," she says. "Scott, you were his family."

"What about you, Sherry?"

She presses a finger to my lips. "To my surprise, Jason left me a little something. His lawyer, Lucinda, came by the day after he died and gave me the paper work. He already had the account set up in my name."

"Is it enough?"

"Too much, actually."

I figure this is as good a time as any to ask a question that's been nagging me.

"What about Lucinda, Sherry? What was she to Jason?"

She smiles. "She was like another sister to him. With his real sister, Mary, living in Kentucky, he needed someone to look after. I think he related to her because she was alone and trying to discover who she really was too."

I nod.

"She loved him very much and there were times that I wished he would fall in love with her and stop worrying over me."

We sit there in silence for a few minutes.

"What are you going to do now, Sherry?"

She smiles. "I don't know, Scott. Maybe I'll finally start living my own life."

"Here in Franklin?"

"Of course. This is my home. I think it's the best place to start."

"What about Jason's family's farm?" I ask.

"I haven't been out there in years. He moved out there quite a while back because his work shop was there, but that was after he and I split. My guess is Mary will get it. You might ask Lucinda."

I lean over and kiss her on the forehead. "I want you to be happy, Sherry. Jason would have wanted you to be happy too, even..."

"Even if what?" she asks.

I know I probably shouldn't say anything but this has gone on long enough. Too many hearts have been broken and it's time to start the healing. "Even if it's with one of his best friends."

"What?" she says, her voice filled with confusion.

"Sherry, Pat is in love with you."

THIRTEEN

Sherry left shortly after my revelation about Pat. She didn't say much, just thanked me for letting her know. She was tired and said she was going home and try to sleep for a few hours. I asked if she wanted me to take her but she declined. She kissed me goodnight and said she would see me at the funeral. I hope she meant it.

I glance at my watch, five-thirty a.m. No point in going to bed now. It occurs to me I haven't checked my e-mail recently, so I grab my laptop and log on. Five e-mails occupy my inbox, three business, one note from the boys saying they miss me, and the last is a note from Melanie.

Scott,

I'm so sorry to hear about Jason. You, Pat and he were so close, like brothers. It was never dull being around the three of you. I know you're hurting now, but remember the good times, the togetherness, and the friendship. Know that he will never truly be gone as long as he's in your heart.

I wish I could be there, but sadly cannot. But know that I am with you in spirit, and know that if you need me, I'm just a phone call away.

All my love,
Melanie

I reply with a simple *Thank You,* and know that she'll understand.

It's six o'clock now, so I go into the bathroom, shave, and take a long shower. Afterwards, I put on some shorts, a golf shirt, and some flip-flops, then I hop into the car and drive to Jackson's Cafe.

There isn't a huge crowd at the restaurant, just a few retirees that can't shake starting their day at sunrise. Clarence and Mona have the few patrons under control and ask me if I want to eat in the kitchen while they cook.

I dig into my second stack of pancakes and relay the events of the past twenty-four hours to Clarence and Mona. They listen intently but don't seem too surprised.

"I knew somethin' was wrong with that boy," Clarence says. "He just didn't look good, started gettin' skinny and kind of had that yellow look about him. Darn shame he didn't let anybody know. Everyone in town would have been there for him."

Mona was curiously quiet. I couldn't tell if she was upset or there was something else. She kept cooking.

"Mona?" I ask. "You all right?"

She stops rolling biscuits and slams down the rolling pin. "*I* knew he was sick, okay. I knew and I didn't tell anyone because he asked me not to." She starts crying and Clarence hands her a dishcloth. "I loved that boy like he was my own, just like I loved you, Scott, and Pat and Sherry, and Mignonne. I loved all of you kids and couldn't stand the way you all had grown apart...but Jason...he was special. All of his family, except his sister, were dead and all of his friends had moved on. It was like he was an orphan and well..."

Clarence gently touches his wife's shoulder. "It's all right, Honey."

She continues. "I started taking him his meals every morning and night when he started remodeling over at Lucinda's. He would work all day without eating if I didn't make him do it. And it just sort of became a habit." She sits down at the chopping table and wipes her hands on her apron. "He never wanted lunch, said he didn't want to disturb his groove once he got working, but occasionally, when we slowed down here, I would walk over with a piece of pie or cake and a glass of iced tea." Her eyes become vacant. "These last few months I started noticing how much food was left on his plate. He wasn't eating it, just picking really so he could tell me he liked it." She dabs her eyes with the dishcloth. "I finally drug the truth out of him. He told me he couldn't really taste things anymore and that he hated for me to keep wasting food on him every day. After that I started taking him oatmeal in the morning and soup at night. I figured even if he couldn't taste it, it would keep his strength up."

Clarence squats beside her and places his hand on her knee. "Why didn't you tell me, Mona. I would've helped."

"I know you would have, but he asked me not to tell any one. He said there was nothing that could be done and he didn't want anybody frettin' over him. He told me he had made peace with himself and with God and he wanted people to remember him as he was, as a fun, caring, artistic man, not some dying invalid. I'm sorry but I respected his wishes."

I join them and we hug and cry. A few minutes later the front door bell tinkles and Clarence and Mona both re-assumed their positions in the kitchen as if nothing has happened, and I know it's time for me to go. I have an appointment with a rock wall and a letter.

"Thanks for breakfast. I'll see you guys later."

Mona comes over and hugs me again. "Don't eat a big lunch. We'll bring food to the funeral home."

"Yes, ma'am."

I leave Jackson's Cafe, go back to the hotel and change into khaki slacks, a white button down shirt, and a blue blazer. The tie goes into my jacket pocket. It's the most dressed up I've been in months. Dress code for a funeral in Hawaii is a *nice* tropical shirt and long pants.

The drive to my destination isn't a long one, maybe a mile and a half from Clarence and Mona's place, three miles from the hotel. Many times my friends and I made the trip from our neighborhood to downtown Franklin. Feet and bicycles were the vehicles of choice back then since none of us were old enough to drive. I drive slowly, passing many familiar houses and yards, trying to remember how things were then and seeing how they've changed now.

I soon pass my Aunt Katie's house. It's painted a different color, but the big front porch looks the same. I wonder if the new owners are similar to Aunt Katie, and if they also buy short, squat, Christmas trees that are wider than tall, and have a fake fire in the hearth that is really just a red light bulb with Santa sitting on top of plastic logs. Aunt Katie was an original. She passed a long time ago, but she will always be remembered for her boisterous personality, tacky decorations, and obnoxious dog, Brutus. I'm sorry my children never got to meet her, because they would have thought she was very cool.

Berry's Circle Drive is still there, a small paved circle surrounded by five homes. Many summer nights when we were little, my Mom and Dad would take all of us neighborhood kids down there to ride bikes.

Most of the homes on this stretch have kept their nostalgic appearance, some have modernized a bit with swimming pools or bigger driveways. I come to the split in the road, take a left, and slow down as I pass the second house on the right, the house I grew up in. Basically it looks the same, maybe a new piece of lattice here, a new flowerbed there. Memories flash through my mind like strobe light pulses and I don't know how to feel…sentimental, sad, or joy? Fifteen years of my life were spent in that house where there were so many memories, so many stories, so much love.

I drive on about a hundred and fifty yards to where Henry's Market used to be and to my surprise it's still there. It seems smaller than I remembered, but looking back I guess it never was that big of a place. I park my car, get out, and stretch. The walls of the store look as if they still have the same white wash on them and I stroll over to see if our initials are still scratched on the sidewall facing the railroad tracks. Mr. Henry gave us permission to do it saying that we were the most regular customers he had so we deserved a bit of distinction. I rub the wall where I think the initials were carved but nothing is there but smooth paint. A train whistle blows and I turn to watch the steel beast pass by, rattling the ground, cars, and the building itself. How many pennies did we place on those tracks over the years? A thought hits me and it makes me sad. My sons have never put a penny on a train track. There are no trains like this in Hawaii.

"My goodness," the voice comes from behind. "Are my eyes playing tricks on me or is that little Scott Sawyer in my parking lot?"

I turn and look into the kind eyes of Mr. Henry.

"Mr. Henry?" I can't believe he's still alive. We figured he was in his seventies when we were little and that would make him around one hundred and ten by now. "It's so good to see you." I reach out to shake his hand and he pulls me in for a hug.

"Land sakes, boy." He raises his eyes. "You've done grown up through your hair."

We both laugh and he invites me inside.

"Bobby!" he calls into the back of the store and a teenage kid comes out of the storeroom.

"Sir?"

"Come here, Bobby. I want you to meet someone."

Bobby comes over and I introduce myself.

He gives me a firm handshake. "Pleased to meet you, Mr. Sawyer," he smiles.

I'm glad to know there are some teenagers who still know how to greet people.

"Scott," Mr. Henry says. "This here's my great grandson, fourth generation Henry to work in the store."

I can tell he's proud of the young man and I would be too.

"Bobby," he continues. "Scott here is one of my longest running customers. Been coming here for…" He looks over at me and I can see that his mind isn't quite as sharp as it used to be.

"Including today," I offer. "Thirty-nine years."

"Thirty-nine years," he whispers. "Heck, I should be retired," he guffaws. Bobby and I exchange a glance and smile, both knowing that Mr. Henry won't ever retire. He will die right here in this store if he has anything to say about it.

Bobby returns to the stockroom and I grab a soda and a bag of peanuts. Mr. Henry asks about my family and if I ever see any of the old neighborhood folks. I respond as accurately as I can and tell him that, in fact, I have seen quite a few locals in the past two days. We discuss how Franklin has changed and then we finally reminisce about Jason and share a prayer together at the checkout counter.

"Tell me about the old neighborhood, Mr. Henry," I say.

He takes off his glasses and begins cleaning the lens with the corner of his work apron. "Well, Scott, other than the houses and yards, there's not much of the old neighborhood there."

"None of the families live there anymore?"

"Not really," he says with a shake of his head. "But there's some good people living there. Sadly there aren't many kids." He suddenly perks up. "Except for at your old place."

"Really?"

"Yep. A nice family from Michigan moved in there about ten years ago. They got a boy, ten, and a little girl, I'd say she's around eight." He gives a chuckle. "Yeah, they come in every Saturday and get a treat, not like you all who came in every afternoon after school and Saturdays when y'all were mowing yards." He puts his glasses back on and scratches his chin. "Yeah, folks in town think of my place as more of a novelty now rather than a grocery store."

I nod knowing exactly what he means.

"Hey, Mr. Henry. Would it be all right if I left my car here and walked up to the old neighborhood?"

"Sure thing." He offers an understanding smile. "Take your time."

"Thanks." I buy another drink and a candy bar and head up the road, passing my destination and wandering a little farther to my old house. I take out my cell phone and snap a picture of the front porch I spent so many days and nights on playing ping-pong, marbles, or just hanging out with the neighbor kids on the swing.

"Can I help you?" comes a sweet voice from the side of the house.

I glance over and see a pretty young woman on her knees in a flowerbed near the side porch.

"I'm terribly sorry," I say. "I didn't see you there."

She stands and brushes the dirt from her shorts. "It's fine. You're not casing the house, are you?"

"Not at all. Just reminiscing. I used to live here."

"Really?" She walks over." I'm Sara Vaughn."

"Scott Sawyer." I shake her hand and her head tilts a bit.

"The author?" she asks.

I'm almost afraid to answer figuring I'll get another, *I like your wife's books better,* but I take the high road and give a simple reply of, "Yes."

"I like your writing style," she says with a smile. "It's very authentic and really pulls me into the story with the descriptions and dialogue. Sometimes, I feel like you're in my head and heart and say just what I would in those situations."

"That's very sweet, Sara. Please tell me you're a literary critic."

"Not hardly," she shrugs. "Just a well-read high school English teacher."

"Who is not in school today?"

She laughs. "I'm playing hooky."

"Sounds good."

She lifts her hand to her forehead and brushes away some loose hair strands. "So, what about you? Why are you here in front of my house? Research maybe?"

"No, I really used to live here, 126 Lewisburg Avenue."

"You're kidding."

"Nope. I lived in this house for fifteen years, then we moved out to Highway 96 in nineteen-seventy-nine." I guess she knows what I'm thinking.

"You want to go inside?"

"I wouldn't want to put you out."

"Promise me an autographed copy of your next book?"

"Done."

"Come on."

I follow her around to the back and she shows me the things she has done in the four years she's lived here and then asks me how things have changed. As far as the yard goes everything is familiar. The barn-like garage is gone and there is now a privacy fence in the back, but otherwise it's the same. The hedges, pecan tree, and magnolia are still standing. And the patio my mother slaved over for several years still covers the courtyard and winds around the house. I laugh out loud and Sara asks why.

"Every couple of months Mom would save enough money to buy a hundred bricks and she would complete another section of patio or walkway. I always felt it was therapeutic for her, digging, smoothing, and laying the bricks as if she were constructing an outdoor mosaic. The bricks, ivy bed, and tool shed were all pieces of the puzzle and she placed all of the pieces just right. She was so proud when she finished and loved the fact that so many of us kids hung out here under the magnolia tree." I walk over to the crawlspace door. "I remember one summer Mom and Dad wanted part of the crawlspace dug out deep enough so an adult could stand under the house. Dad wanted to plant some potatoes under there and have room for storage. He told us that our entire yard had been built over part of the Civil War battlefield and that many relics and possibly some money were probably under the house. We had found a few bullets and a confederate breastplate before while digging in the dirt, so several of us guys started digging and before getting very deep we started finding change, quarters, dimes, nickels."

"Really?" Sara said, intrigued. "From the Civil War?"

"Not hardly, but in our excitement of finding money we didn't inspect the coins that thoroughly. It was a couple of hours later that my friend, Pat, noticed the quarters were dated nineteen-seventy-two." A wonderful memory comes to me. "I remember we were digging one night and Mom came out onto the patio with a tray of Kool-aid and cookies and she had the portable television, black and white, of course. She told us all to come out of the crawlspace and get a snack. We did and she placed us all where we could see the TV. My brother finally asked her what she was doing and she said an important event was about to happen and even though we might not relate to it now, later on we would understand."

Sara looks confused. "What was it?"

"Nixon's resignation speech."

"Wow."

"Yeah. She did the same thing with Elvis' televised Hawaii concert."

"Were you an Elvis fan?"

"Have been ever since," I reply with a curl of my lip.

"Come on inside."

I step through the back door and close my eyes. The scent, feel, and aura of the house descends upon me like a tidal wave and I feel a bit light headed. I open my eyes and a tear trickles down my cheek.

"You okay, Scott?"

"Very."

She takes me around the house and shows me pictures of her children and tells me how much they love Mr. Henry. Then, she asks me a million questions about the history of the house and she wants to know some of my fondest memories and if there is anything I could tell her about the house that no one else would know. I didn't have any secrets about the house but I tell her about the fun and love our family shared over the years and I tell her one of my favorite Sawyer Christmas stories.

* * *

A couple of days before Christmas Mom had gone shopping, leaving Dad with me and my brother, Tim. We were already out of school and desperately counting the minutes, hours, and days before Santa, and Dad was doing his best to keep us occupied so we would stop worrying him to death about the gifts under the tree. He had given us a puzzle or a game and we were sitting on our bed playing.

After a while, he came into our room and started messing with us, wrestling a bit and saying he was king of the bed, then, suddenly, he took off running towards the living room, clearly a challenge for us to chase him and we were up to the task. Our house was really cool in the fact that every room connected to the next room and you could make a complete circle around the entire house.

A side note here. For several Christmases, my grandmother crocheted Tim and me house slippers. They were usually a funky color, soft and fuzzy, and great for sliding on hardwood floors. Since it was Christmas, she always put jingle bells on them and for some reason our dachshund, Hot Dog, hated those slippers. I don't know if it was the bells or the fuzz, but every time we wore them and moved quickly Hot Dog chased us with a vengeance. Any other time we ran through the house she would ignore us or look at us like we were idiots. She was rather lazy and incredibly big for a miniature dachshund, three feet long and forty-two pounds.

This particular night, Dad took off, Tim followed, and I brought up the rear, or so I thought. Hot Dog was quickly on my fuzzy heels, snarling and nipping as she ran. On the second lap around the interior of the house, I heard a commotion ahead but couldn't see around the corner. When I made the turn I saw the cause of the ruckus. Too late. Dad had apparently not been able to make the turn on his feet and he slipped and slid into the end table that held an antique lamp and more importantly a large brandy snifter that Mom used as a Christmas decoration. Each year she filled it with angel's hair material and placed a porcelain Mary and Jesus figure inside. The snifter hadn't fallen but it was teetering near the edge. Tim had tried to stop as well, but the slippers were his undoing and he did a face dive into Dad. Still the table stood and the glassware was safe. I tried a different approach. I figured if I shifted all of my weight back, maybe I could stop my momentum. Wrong. My fuzzy heels hit the hardwood like a penguin's butt on ice and, WHAM, down I went and slid right into Tim's back. The snifter wobbled horribly and we just knew it was coming down. I covered my head and Tim screamed but nothing happened. The glass came to a safe rest with a third of the base dangerously edging over the side. We all released a collective sigh of relief that gradually became raucous laughter.

Slowly, we began to untie the pretzel of bodies we had become, but our act was premature. First, we heard the growling, followed by the barking of an excited dog who smelled victory. We had forgotten Hot Dog. Here she came, a snarling, sniveling, black ball of canine terror, rounding the corner with all four feet touching hardwood at the same time. Forty-two pounds of a flabby dachshund with long toenails hit smooth finished oak at a blazing two miles an hour and the propulsion of dog fat was too great for the stubby paws to overcome.

It was similar to one of those plot altering moments in a movie, where the director would have run the scene in slow motion. The feet slipping to the left. The tail curling to the right. The eyes large and white. The large, fat-rippled body flattening like a seal on an ice floe as it splats against the floor. She was shooting towards us like a torpedo and suddenly I understood the terror American sailors must have felt when they saw the cylindrical missiles launched towards their ships by the Japanese and Germans. And Hot Dog, being the greedy, awesome eating machine that she was, actually stuck her tongue out and tried to lick up a popcorn morsel dropped earlier in the evening while she skidded towards certain doom. Suddenly, the world went silent and darkness descended as if time had stopped. But it hadn't, and I was witness to the horror of canine hurtling into human, thus setting off the series of events that would haunt us for many Christmases to come.

It gets a bit foggy after that, but what I vaguely recall is Hot Dog's nose hitting my chest, pushing my butt further into Tim's face, snapping his head back into Dad's shoulder, which then hit the table. The lamp was heavy enough to withstand the barrage, but the finely blown brandy snifter leapt two feet from the table as if shot from a catapult, clearing our piled of bodies. For a moment it seemed as if it might land softly and safely on the large shag area rug, but that moment was fleeting as glass met hardwood. I had no idea that glass could shatter into so many pieces. The snifter splintered into such small shards I swear parts returned to sand form. Undoubtedly, it was one of the most horrifying and cool things I had ever witnessed.

We stood and surveyed the carnage before us. Jesus, of course, had been saved, entangled in the glorious angel hair. But Mary, love her heart, had been thrown clear of the cushioning armor that protected our Savior and lay before us a broken and be-headed figurine.

Tim and I panicked while Hot Dog fled for safety under the claw-footed bathtub. Dad, however, being the always cool Big Kahuna, devised a story. We would tell Mom that the brandy snifter must have had a crack in it and probably shattered because of the severe temperature change outside.

"But what about Mary's head?" Tim and I asked simultaneously.

Dad's reply was genius. "Superglue."

Okay, it wasn't genius. In fact it was quite stupid, but it was the best we could come up with. We glued her head back on but couldn't figure out how to cover the scar. Unless we could pass her off as *Frankenstein Jesus' mother*, or *Mary from a western version of the Christmas story*, where Mary acquired her neck scar after she had been saved at the last minute from a hanging, then this wasn't going to work unless…

We swept and vacuumed as much glass as we could and placed Jesus and *Diva Mary*, who now sported a blue furry boa, directly on the table wrapped in Angel's Hair. Mom came home a few hours later, and of course, noticed immediately.

Several versions of the story were practiced, but when faced with Mom's interrogation eyes, Dad, Timmy, and I gave up and pointed our accusatory fingers at the guilty party…Hot Dog.

* * *

Sara and I both laugh for quite a while and I tell a few more stories over a cup of tea. She asks me to stay for lunch, and I tell her I would love to, but I need to get going. I tell her about Jason and she understands. After taking a few more pictures of the house to show the boys I head out the door, promising Sara I will send an autographed copy of my next book to this address.

"Unless you're going to be finished with that book in the next month," she says. "You'll have to send it to another address."

"How come," I ask.

She bites her lip and explains. "Sadly, my husband's company is transferring us to Virginia."

"Have you sold this house already?"

"Nope. That's why I'm playing hooky today. I'm trying to get the flower beds pretty to put it on the market."

"Kind of late in the game, isn't it?"

She shakes her head. "This move came up suddenly, and it's a good job, so off we go."

"Well, I wish you all my best, Sara. It has been an absolute pleasure meeting you, and thanks..."

"For what?"

"For the stroll down memory lane."

She gives me her new address and cell phone number, then we hug and she says she will pray for all of us.

I leave Sara and make the short walk a couple of houses down the road to the special place Jason has referred to, the stone wall in front of Ms. Hardison's old house. She was the sweetest lady and best babysitter in the neighborhood and, never having any kids of her own, she loved having us hang out on her wall and playing in her lot across the street.

When we were kids, we figured Ms. Hardison had been somewhere between ninety-two and one-hundred-forty-seven years old and on the wall in her hallway we swore she had a high school picture with Methuselah in it.

It's both sorrowful and comforting to be here.

I walk over to my former favorite spot, brush the dirt away, sit down, and begin.

FOURTEEN

"The sky darkens as the heart breaks."
"Bitter tears fall from sorrowful eyes that have seen into the soul."
"Love harkens from the inner self of another."

These are the types of made up lines spoken by characters from the kind of stories my wife teaches and writes about. They are deep and thought provoking but don't seem realistic coming from the characters in my stories. I do like lines like these. In fact, there is one that resides in my heart now, and it's not from a book, play, or movie. It is, in fact, from a friend of mine, written after the loss of her grandfather.

"Time is not allowed to stop. Hearts only come to a halt when the mind is ready to be released away from the physical window."

I ponder the relevance of this wisdom in my current situation, having returned to my past after such a long absence. Time is indeed not allowed to stop, yet more than thirty years later, here I sit on the old stone wall where so many summer days and after school hours were spent, discussing all of the things kids find relative and crucial.

I look at Jason's envelope, then I glance around and am disappointed in how the old neighborhood has changed. Where once there were spacious back yards, welcoming porches, and patios, now stand fences, chain-link boundaries serving as reminders that the society we live in has become un-trusting and fearful. Neighbors are no longer considered 'friends'. Instead, they are nonchalant acquaintances you wave to while backing out of the driveway or taking out the trash.

What's happened to people? Where are their hearts? Where is their concern for fellow humans? And where is their common sense?

Franklin, Tennessee, has grown from the sleepy droll community of my youth, to an overpriced mecca of debt ridden yuppies and celebrities wanting to retain a sense of their humble beginnings by owning a half a million dollar house in the *country*.

I guess that I can understand what they're feeling. While my adult life has been a success both financially and personally, there is still an emptiness...a longing for something I haven't had since...well since I left Franklin...a sense of belonging and warmth that one can't really develop in the conglomerate of wealth and power that go hand in hand in the setting of a large city.

Across the street is the field where I once hit so many baseballs, caught millions of fire-flies, and experienced so many lessons of life. We had wiener roasts every weekend there. The fire was always built on top of the pitcher's mound and after it burnt down we would add dirt and press it down. That pitcher's mound was perfect, and I had always felt it would rival any in the majors. It's overgrown with weeds now, and the field itself has a *for sale by owner* sign in front of it.

On this hot, sticky morning, I check my watch, eleven o'clock, two hours before I have to drive to the funeral and say farewell to Jason. Tragic and sad he is gone so young, with so much seemingly going on in his life, but car wrecks and cancer have no age requirement and no emotion.

If people would only realize how fragile our lives are and enjoy them to the fullest while they can. I have made it a habit to always try and tell the special people in my life I love them every chance I get, because you never know when it could be the last time.

A sob escapes and tears come. I wonder…do these tears come from grief of losing my friend or regret for never coming back to see him or any of the other people I abandoned when I went to find myself? Deep down I know the answer. I cry because I can't remember the last time I told Jason I loved him.

I reach for my handkerchief, then remember I gave it to Nancy and forgot to put another one in my pocket. I take a few deep breaths instead and try to compose myself. Questions keep popping into my brain. What were the reasons I left? Did I accomplish my goal by moving away? Have I discovered myself and what truly makes me complete as a person, husband, or father? True, I have a wonderful wife and two fantastic children, but do I have the simple things in my world that make up a *life?*

We had so much growing up. I'm not talking about money or material possessions; those were in short supply. I'm talking about blessed, rich gifts such as love, compassion, friendship and togetherness. It was a time when everyone in the neighborhood looked out for everyone else as if we were one big happy family. The type you see on television and think *no one is really like that,* but we were. There were no *only* children in our neighborhood. Every kid had eight or nine brothers and sisters and at least six sets of parents.

It's getting hot, but soon a cloud slips lazily in front of the sun and a cool breeze whips some dried grass clippings across my lap bringing a smile to my face as I drift back in time to those wonderful summers of my youth where every day and night were considered an adventure, no matter what happened. So many nights of playing spotlight, hide and seek, and bicycle tag, or telling ghost stories while sitting on the trampoline, and camping out in the old field we used as our personal sports arena.

The sun reappears and after a few minutes I feel my face start to burn, but I can't leave. Instead, I pick up my drink, candy bar and the envelope, stand, then walk down a bit to where a walnut tree shades the wall and make myself comfortable again by unbuttoning a couple of my shirt buttons and kicking off my shoes.

I pop open the drink I bought earlier, scan the neat row of houses and lawns, then wonder why I decided that this life wasn't what I wanted. When did simple and comfortable become offensive? I laugh, realizing of course that I'm being silly. Those things were never offensive, just not terribly exciting in your early twenties.

I realize, of course, what I'm doing... putting off the inevitable future by reminiscing in the past. It's time to do what I came here to do. The manilla envelope feels heavy, but I can't tell if it's from actual weight or the thought of the sadness that the envelope could contain. The flap is sealed and fastened so I pull out my pocket knife and gently cut through the glue then straighten the brass prongs. I slide my knife back into my pocket, then reach inside for the papers Jason has left me to read. Instead of loose paper, I pull free two letter size envelopes and a packet of pages bound with a paperclip. The envelopes are numbered 1 and 3, in order to be opened. The packet of pages has a number 2 tucked under the paperclip so I put it and the envelope marked number three aside.

From inside the envelope marked *read first*, I pull out three hand written pages. It's definitely Jason's handwriting, a distinct scribble made up of a series of loops and jags bordering on hieroglyphics. The letter begins as most do. Well, maybe not.

Dear Scott:

If you are reading this, the reason is obvious. Either I'm dead or I am really drunk and have posted this on the internet. Most likely, it's the former, since by now you probably know I was sick and therefore not drinking anymore. I'm sorry for not telling you by the way. At the time it didn't seem important. But I realize now that it was selfish of me.

I hope this letter finds you well, though I know that is silly to say. You're a rich, best-selling author, who lives in Paradise, and has the most wonderful wife anyone could ask for. I'll admit that I was always a bit jealous and envious of you, pal, but to be honest, I wouldn't trade places with you.

I found my happiness. Sure, I didn't realize it until later in my life, but I discovered that time isn't a factor when you're truly happy, or when you know your time is limited. The only reason I wish I had more time is so I could tell all the people I hurt or disappointed that I'm truly sorry…and so that I could tell so many people how much they meant to me and that I love them. And the first person I want to tell…is you.

I never understood why, but you became my friend when others wouldn't. You gave me hope, guidance, and a kick in the pants whenever I needed it. For that, you always were and will always be my best friend. I know we haven't seen or spoken to each other for quite some time but that doesn't matter. You are a part of me and I will take that part with me wherever God decides I'm going.

I love you, Scott. You will always be my best friend. I hope that because of that friendship you will grant me a few favors. First, I need you to tell Sherry that I loved her more than life itself, and I wish her all of the joy and happiness she deserves. She put so much of her life into me and I gave very little back. I am so sorry for that. I was wrong to push her away when I

found out I was sick, but didn't want her living with my illness everyday. After all I had done to her in the past, I had hoped she would finally get so mad at me that she would move on to a better life. Instead, all I did was break her heart, over and over again. I know I can't ever take any of that back but I hope I can help her find her true happiness.

Second, I need you to talk to Pat for me. In the last few years, he and I...well...we had a falling out and I always regretted the things I said to him. But after a while it just seemed too late to mend the fence so I need your wisdom on this.

The reason for our falling out was simple. He was in love with Sherry and deep down I knew she was in love with him. I blew up, and to this day I still don't know why. I knew that Sherry and I should never get married. I loved her but we weren't ever really meant to be together. Our relationship was a lot like beer and wine, good to have at a party but never in the same glass.

Pat was good to and for Sherry. He remembered important dates and things about her and always knew the right thing to say and how to make her feel good about herself. Truth is, it was actually fun watching the two of them together, laughing and picking on each other.

I know that both of them are hurting now and I've been the cause of that hurt for far too long.

Scott, please tell Pat that I'm sorry, that I love him, and that if the feelings are still there, he should tell Sherry how he feels and not waste another minute of his life without her. Tell him that if I could have one more minute with him, it would be to tell him that he is the better man and the better friend.

Now for the third and final favor. Open the packet marked 2, read the note, then move on to the envelope marked number 3.

The letter ends there so I do as he asks. There is another hand written note under the paperclip on the packet marked 2.

>   *A few years ago, I found this in my closet. I had forgotten so much of this, but when I reread it…that moment in my life, our lives, came flooding back, and the memories of that experience are what have guided me through these final years. The serenity and peace of that day and those beautiful creatures have brought balance into my life and taught me the most valuable lesson of my life.*
>
>   *Do you remember this quote? "Could it be, that even though he was way off his destination, he was happy and content because he and his friends had found a nice pond in which to soak their feet and catch a few minnows, and that as long as the path eventually led home, it didn't matter how long it took to get there?" Now look at the packet.*

I pull the note off the papers and can't believe my eyes. Scrawled across the top of the page in my handwriting is the title of the short story I wrote when I was sixteen years old: *THE SUMMER OF THE PINK FLAMINGOES.*

My first thoughts of becoming a writer came after I wrote this story but I had been too scared to show it to anyone, thinking it might make me sound like a wus. But finally I gave it to Jason and he had kept it all these years. On the right side of the title in red marker was a note that said:

Now open envelope marked 3.

I reach over, flip open the envelope, and inside is a picture. A picture that takes me back to a better time. A picture that makes me…remember.

* * *

The Summer of 1978 began like every summer before, nasty hot weather, tons of chores, and not enough hours in the day. Within the first week my best friends and I, Pat Wilson and Jason Maler, were already avoiding our parent's list of chores they left on the kitchen table most mornings before they went to work. We would get out of bed, dress, brush our teeth, and scoot out the back door without breakfast. That way, we could honestly tell our Mothers that, *no, we hadn't seen the list on the kitchen table.* Deep down I always felt that she knew we were doing this, but she played along, knowing that there was no fun in trying to outsmart your parents if they didn't fall for it every once in a while. We would then go to a neighbor's house, bum a biscuit and jelly from one of our friends' mothers, then hop on our bikes and take off.

Most of our summer days were spent fishing in the Harpeth River. It was just a couple of miles down the road by bicycle, or closer if you cut through backyards and walked the railroad tracks. It was overgrown and weedy but we had made the trip so many times that we had pressed a flat grass trail to our favorite spot or spots. I say spots because there were a multitude to choose from. If your fishing luck was bad at the riverbank, then conveniently located over an embankment by the river was a small pond that had a few catfish, crawdads, and tadpoles swimming in it. Many treks were made over that embankment, back and forth depending on which water held the magical hot spot that particular day.

Money was scarce at that point so fishing bait was hard to come by. Pack's Mini-Mart downtown had night crawlers and crickets, but bugs were expensive. Sure, we cut grass and raked yards, but that money was for important things such as going to the movies, or buying records, or a cool t-shirt.

So we found our fishing bait the old fashioned way, we caught it in the fields surrounding the water. You *could* scrape the soft dirt with a stick or rock and occasionally find a juicy worm, but mostly, all you had to do was walk into the overgrown grass, smack the ground with your flat hand, and a grasshopper would pop up ninety-nine percent of the time.

For many hours on those magnificent days, we would sit on a fallen tree trunk, dangle our feet in the Harpeth's cool water, and just watch the river flow by. Sometimes we would make up stories about the things that floated past, such as trash, leaves and branches. About where they had come from? How far would they go? Would we ever travel as far as the paper cup bobbing across the ripples? Was there a kid somewhere upstream doing the exact same thing and sending these small flotilla our way?

These were glorious, simple times spent together where nothing in the world seemed very important and no problem was too difficult to bear.

I awoke one particularly spectacular Saturday morning to a phenomenal sunrise. It had rained the night before and the world sparkled as the sun crested over the rooftops. The trees and yards were lush and green and the birds sang beautifully as if their songs were summoning the glistening golden rays down from Heaven. I opened my bedroom window and took a deep whiff of the morning. Today smelled different. Something exciting was in the air.

I grabbed my shorts and t-shirt from the bedpost, slipped on my old sneakers and hopped out of the window. I knew it was earlier than our usual fishing time, but the day was too nice to waste. Being Saturday morning, I knew Mom and Dad would sleep late and wouldn't even miss me before ten o'clock.

I went to the garage and grabbed my fishing pole, net, and bucket, then headed for Jason's house. Pat's house was closer but

Jason felt more included and not so much an afterthought if I got him first. It was silly, especially for a guy, to be this way, but Pat and I had brought him into our circle and we wanted to keep him there.

I gently pecked on Jason's window, not wanting to wake his parents and got no response. I tried again a little louder, still nothing. Growing more frustrated as minutes of fabulous fishing time slipped past, I raised my fist to do some serious knocking.

"I wouldn't do that," came from behind.

I turned and there stood Jason, fishing pole at the ready.

"Did you see that sunrise, Scott?" he gushed. "It was awesome."

I nodded and smiled. Jason always appreciated nature's beauty, probably more so than me or Pat. He occasionally drew some pretty good pictures of landscapes, beaches and animals, but didn't do it often. I had a picture of his framed in my room. It was a pencil sketch of an owl and its baby that had been hanging out in the old barn near his parent's farm. I thought it was one of the coolest things I'd ever seen and he gave it to me for my last birthday.

We headed to Pat's and knew immediately that something was amiss because the kitchen and bathroom lights were already on. Since his entire family seemed to be awake, we decided to knock on the door, hoping his mom might have made one of her special weekend sweet rolls. But alas, it was not to be. Pat answered the door and on his face was the vacant look of someone who had received terrible news. And indeed he had.

Tragedy had struck the children in his family...all the kids needed new church shoes, so they would spend the entire morning making the trip to Nashville to Utopia Shoe Store. A kid being told that he had to spend a beautiful summer Saturday at the shoe store was the equivalent, I'm sure, of the feeling draftees must have felt when they were summoned to war.

Jason and I sure felt sorry for Pat having to face a day of boredom, agony, and most likely a grounding at some point, because what self respecting kid could be expected to go a whole day in a shoe store with siblings and not do something bad.

Jason and I said a sympathetic prayer for him, grabbed our fishing poles, and headed for the water.

This morning, we decided to hike the railroad tracks to the bridge and, as usual, I bet Jason a soda that I could walk longer on a single track than he could, but he didn't bite. Pat and I had both taken what amounted to several cases of drinks from Jason on that bet because of his total lack of coordination and balance.

"Oh, come on," I pleaded. "It's gonna be hot today and I'm going to be really thirsty." Jason usually ignored these taunts, but he couldn't turn away from a challenge if you kept egging him on. "Seriously, Jason. There's got to be a first time for everything. Today may be the day you win."

"Fine!" he said with flair. "You're going down."

We each hopped on a rail and headed forward. I glanced over occasionally and noticed that Jason wasn't bobbing and weaving like usual. Today, he actually seemed to be one with the rail and that made me nervous.

"Hey, Jason? Are you breathing in or out on each step?"

"Don't start with the mind games, Scott. It won't work today," he said with a laugh and actually sped up. Then he took off, walking very quickly, leaving me in the dust. I tried to speed up and within two steps my foot slipped off the iron balance beam.

"Woo-hoo!" I heard him shout. "You owe me a Coke, buddy-boy." He was dancing on the rail and laughing.

"How in the world…?" I sighed.

"Just talented, I guess." He put his hands on his hips and looked to the sky. "It's gonna be a special day today, Scott. I can feel it."

I walked by and shoved him, then stopped and turned back. He was still on the rail.

"What the…?"

Jason just smiled then tried to lift his foot. "Uh-oh," he gushed. Then he tried to lift the other foot even harder. "Oh, man."

I said to him, "What did you do?"

"Okay, I cheated. When you weren't looking I sprayed stickum on my shoes."

"You're kidding?"

"No." He pulled the can out of his pocket and showed it to me. "Guess I stood in one place too long and it stuck for real."

I couldn't help but get tickled, then he started laughing and before you know it we had a full fledged case of the giggles and no clue of how to get him unstuck.

HOOOONNKK!!

We both spun around and Jason nearly fell.

"Train!" we both shouted. I grabbed Jason's leg and pulled frantically but to no avail.

"Crap, Scott. What do we do?"

The train crept around the bend and honked again.

"Step out of your shoes," I hollered.

He pulled free of one but couldn't get out of the other.

"Oh, jeez. Double knot." he cried.

The train edged closer and closer. There was no other choice. I pulled out my pocket knife and flipped it open.

"No, Scott. These are twenty-five dollar Keds. My mom will freak if you cut the strings."

"Are you out of your mind?" I said with shock.

The train was right on top of us now. I bent over and sliced neatly through the shoestrings, cutting the Keds logo neatly in half, and yanked with all my might, pulling Jason right over on top of me.

Above me I heard, "Stupid kids!" As we fell, I saw the train engineer leaning out of his window with his fist raised. I waved, knowing that was all I could do.

I glanced over at Jason and saw him sitting up with the dumbest expression I had ever seen on his face. His eyes were huge and his mouth hung open in a perfect O. I reached over and snapped my fingers in front of his face.

As if on cue he spurted, "That was awesome! Man! I told you today was gonna be special."

We both got up and brushed the loose gravel from our clothes and scraped legs. The tail end of the train was rolling by now and Jason stood there anxiously waiting to see the fate of his prized sneakers. When the last wheel rolled by, it wasn't pretty.

"Oh, man," he said as he tried to pry one of the flattened tennis shoes from the rail. "It's still stuck." We yanked and yanked but couldn't free the shoe and there was no sign of the other.

I shook my head. "Looks like you're barefootin' today, buddy."

After a few more tries, we abandoned the shoe and headed on for the river. The day was too wonderful to be deterred by loss of footwear.

A quarter mile more and we reached the bridge. There wasn't much traffic, but that wasn't unusual for early Saturday morning. People wouldn't be out and about for a while.

We climbed down the rock ledge to the river, traversed the path for about fifty yards and found our spot on the tree trunk that had fallen on the bank two winters ago.

I sat down and removed my hook snagged safely onto the rod eye, then reached into my pocket and pulled out a fat grasshopper.

"Where'd you get that?" Jason asked.

"He hopped on me when we were walking the trail."

"Lucky."

I laughed too soon because at that very moment the grasshopper got loose and jumped free, so Jason and I both headed for the bushes in search for bait. I was crawling around a particularly prickly blackberry bush when Jason spoke.

"Thanks, Scott."

I raised my head. "What?"

He was standing behind me, looking humbled.

"Thanks for being there for me, for saving me."

"Aw, heck," I answered with a flick of my wrist as I went back to bait hunting. "I don't think you were in any real danger."

"I'm not just talking about today."

I stopped. Jason had a way of reading too much into things and he could get somber very quickly. Pat and I had noticed this soon after we had befriended him. He didn't have many friends and his family was always so busy that he apparently didn't have many opportunities to have real conversations. The best way to handle this was to just let him have his say.

"You're welcome, Jason."

He nodded and disappeared into the brush, then returned. "I mean it."

"I know you do. Let's fish."

Other than the excitement with the train, the morning had been uneventful. We'd been at the river nearly two hours and the fish didn't seem to be interested. The air was getting hot and humid and the wind was still. The only movement came from the muddy Harpeth flowing by with an occasional stick or leaf drifting past. It was nine o'clock and the temperature was already hovering around ninety-two.

I pulled my line from the water and studied the water-logged grasshopper barely hanging by its antennae on my hook. Maybe it was just too hot for a fish to chase a grasshopper. I know I didn't want to go into the brush and catch another one. I dropped the bug back into the water and raised my face towards the blue sky, when suddenly, from behind, I heard the most horrendous screech I'd ever heard. It scared Jason so badly, he dropped his fishing pole into the river, and while that was terribly funny, my curiosity got the best of me, so I jumped up and I ran up the bank to investigate. Jason begged for me to wait, but I just couldn't.

"Fine. If something bad happens to you, don't expect me to take the blame!" Jason truly felt that statement released him from all liability.

I crept through the bushes and pushed away the vines till I reached the edge of the embankment, then dropped on my stomach to peer over the ridge into the pond from where the sound had come. And there *they* were.

The most beautiful, spectacular, and most awkward creatures I had ever laid my eyes on. There must have been thirty of them strutting in the shallow water, bobbing their heads for tiny minnows, and acting as if they owned the place. I blinked a couple of times just to make sure it wasn't the heat playing tricks on me but they were still there. I had only seen them before on TV, or at a zoo, but I knew for a fact that these animals were pink flamingoes. I also knew that they definitely didn't belong in Tennessee.

Jason finally came huffing up the embankment. "Well, I got my pole out of the water, no thanks to you."

"Shhhh."

"Don't shush me," he sighed. "You know what? I can't believe you would risk your life pulling me from in front of a train but then wouldn't help me..."

"Jason, be quiet," I whispered.

He finally noticed the birds, got down on his belly and crawled up beside me. "Oh, my gosh..." he gasped. "What are they doing here?"

"I have no idea," was all I could say.

FIFTEEN

I feel the vibration of my cell phone in my pocket, followed by the annoying *Chicken Dance*, a ring-tone my sons have downloaded.

"This is Scott," I answer.

"Hey, Bud," Pat says. "Where are you?"

"Just a place." The words catch in my throat. I hope Pat didn't notice.

"You okay?" Apparently he had.

"I'm good," I lie. "What are you doing?"

"Having tea with a friend."

"Tea? Pat Wilson is having tea?

"Yeah, tea. This is a sophisticated friend," he laughs.

"Apparently." I'm glad Pat's mood is a bit lighter.

"Come join us?"

The thought of meeting a girl who would be having tea with Pat does arouse my curiosity, but not quite enough.

"I think I'm just going to hang for a while before the funeral."

"Hey, Scott?" he asks with a more serious tone. "You want or *need* some company?"

I think about that, then realize that there are only two people I would want to share this moment with. One of them is in Hawaii and the other one, well, he's the reason I'm here.

"I appreciate it, Pat, but I'm okay. However, there is something I want to talk to you about before the funeral."

"You got it. Call me if you need me."

"Thanks." I click off the phone, pick up the picture again, and gently trace my fingertip across the image of me, Jason, and the flamingoes. I close my eyes and can almost feel their wings flapping overhead...

* * *

Slowly, we stood, crept to the edge of the water, and sat down quietly, careful not to disturb the birds.

At first, they were startled by our appearance and began squawking and flapping their wings but soon fell back into their routine of wading and snipping at tiny fish. For the next couple of hours, we sat there watching them, mesmerized by their presence and their stunning grace and beauty. Then it seemed, after a while, that *they* began watching us as well. Three or four of them cautiously walked within a foot of us. One of them even pecked at Jason's toe. He jumped and I laughed.

Even though we never wore watches in the summertime, you could approximate time either by the location of the sun in the sky, or by the emptiness in your stomach. It was obviously getting later in the day because our appetite alarm clocks were ringing, alerting us that it was lunchtime.

"Dude, I hate to leave but I'm starving," Jason announced. "I'm gonna head back home and eat."

"I can't believe you would leave something like this."

Jason glanced at the birds then back at me. "Sorry, but the stomach calls." He got up.

"Well, are you coming back?" I asked with frustration.

"Sure."

"Then bring me a sandwich…and a camera."

"You got it."

He said he would also go around the neighborhood and round up as many kids as he could, because if no one else saw the birds, they would never believe the two of us. He was right, of course, and off he went. The birds hardly raised their heads as he padded away barefoot.

Jason had been gone about thirty minutes, and it had gotten so hot, that I decided to take a dip. I stood and ever so slowly waded into the water to join the birds. At first they were a bit startled and several of them flapped their wings in protest but soon they seemed to realize that I wasn't going to hurt them and settled down. I poked around with my toes and found a little sink hole about two feet deep and submerged as much of my body in it as I could. Man, did the cool water feel good! No matter how high the thermometer rose during the summer, the water in the pond was always refreshing and cool.

I scanned the flock with wonder till one particular bird caught my eye. He was a bit thinner than the others, a little scruffy, and his feathers seemed to have a mind of their own with several clumps of them sticking out in different directions. They reminded me of my hair in the morning when I first wake up. His head seemed too big for his fuzzy little body, but still, he had managed to perch himself up on one leg and tuck his white face under his pink wing to take a nap. This didn't look very comfortable to me. Personally, I don't think I could sleep like that, but then again, I'm not a pink fuzzy bird.

After a while, most of the birds stepped elegantly towards the bank of the pond in search for more fish in the shallows or for bugs in the wet grass, but my distinctive little friend remained in his spot napping until a small bass broke the surface of the water in pursuit of a dragonfly. The bird's head jerked up; he dropped his lifted leg; then he gracefully spread his wings to their full width. It was the most incredible thing I had ever seen. As awkward and oddly put together as he was, he was strikingly beautiful.

I scratched my head, thinking I had heard that before. Then it hit me. That's what my grandmother said about me, except she used the word handsome instead of beautiful. Finally, I understood what she meant.

Without warning, the bird cautiously stepped forward, lowered his head, cawed, and gave a slight peck at my arm. Instinctively, I pulled away. It scared me a bit but didn't hurt. I think he was just checking me out, so I settled back down in my sinkhole.

He seemed to relax as well, then he raised his slender neck and slowly moved his face within inches of mine. It was time to take a chance. I swallowed hard, then ever-so-slowly, lifted my hand from the water and inched it towards his head. He ducked slightly, then stopped, as if to say, okay, I pecked you, so now you can pet me. My fingers quivered slightly as I moved them closer, then, finally, I touched the brilliantly pink feathers and was amazed how they felt. They were as soft, warm, and fuzzy as my mother's old bath robe.

He then raised his head so that my hand would slip down his neck onto his back. My hand slid down the delicate curve of his neck to his body and I stroked him gently across his back and around his wings. When I reached his belly, he lifted his left leg and scratched the air, just like my dachshund, Hot Dog.

What happened next was unbelievable. In fact, I wouldn't have believed it myself if I hadn't been there.

The flamingo lowered his head, allowing his eyes to meet mine. Like statues, we stayed, staring deeply into each other's eyes. In that quiet, still moment, it was like our minds melded, causing me to feel his calmness and contentment and he my curiosity and wonder.

Then, unexpectedly, I heard shouts and screams coming from the highway. I looked up and saw about fifty people standing on the bridge pointing down at the pond. The birds on the bank were now visible from the highway.

Some of the people had their cameras and were clicking away. Others had decided to invade my and the birds' space by climbing down the rocky ledge, serving them right when two of them tumbled down the gravelly slope into the grass. I didn't wish anybody hurt, but I wanted them to respect these creatures and the relationship I had formed with them.

I glanced back towards the bridge, and that was when I noticed Pat and most of the kids from the neighborhood standing on the bridge. They were cheering and shouting, calling me birdman, and Tarzan, and I admit that I liked it. Jason had made his way down again and was now running towards me.

"I told you I would get everybody," he yelled.

And he had. Good old Jason.

Being quiet birds of the wild, the flamingoes, in no way, liked this loud and rambunctious commotion. They quickly skittered away from the growing crowd. Then, in a glorious flap of pink and white feathery wings, the majestic birds launched into the humid, summer sky and ascended towards the heavens.

All of them, that is, except the bird in front of me. I kept my eyes glued on my new friend as he raised his head and watched his friends go. Then a strange and wonderful thing happened. The flamingo turned his attention back to me, tilted his head sideways...and winked, as if to say, *come with me.*

I smiled in amazement, mesmerized by this creature and his trust of me, a human being he had never seen. Then he did something that will stick with me for the rest of my life. He gracefully lifted his right leg and held it out to me. I could hardly breathe, and at that moment, the world seemed to slow down, almost to a stop. Carefully, I took his foot in my hand, and gently shook it.

He then turned away from me, spread his wings, let out a glorious screech, and flew his beautiful body towards the sky.

I gasped, the air rushing from my lungs as if my new friend needed an extra boost of wind to help him on his way. Slowly I stood and watched him go until he passed over the trees and then...he was gone. It was at that point I realized I was crying, not from sadness or pain, but out of awe and happiness.

Who knows why that glorious creature of God allowed me to share a brief moment of his and his friends' life. Maybe it was because I was young, or that I had been patient, giving him the time to feel comfortable around me. Or maybe, just maybe...it was to let me know that life was bigger than any of us, and no matter what the circumstances...we should just live it.

It was the most unbelievable experience of my life, and because of it, I knew that...one day...I wanted to live where the pink flamingoes lived.

SIXTEEN

And now I do. There are very real pink and white flamingoes within a mile of my Hawaiian home, but I realize now that it's not quite the same.

Again, I glance at the picture Jason has left me and realize that one of the people on the bridge that day made it down to the pond and snapped the photo of the flamingoes circling the pond. He must have squatted down and taken the picture to get an upwards angle. The flamingoes flew in the background and Jason and I stood in the foreground, both of us with our arms lifted towards the sky cheering.

Not so many years later, I had left Franklin, moved to Hawaii, and there I have remained, letting my life drift past as lazily as the flamingoes had let the water trickle around their long legs.

I glance at my watch again. It's time…time to say good-bye to Jason. As I put on my tie and slip on my shoes, a shiver passes through my entire body and a smile forms as I realize something.

At that young age, I had completely misunderstood the flamingo. He hadn't been inviting me to come away with him to his tropical paradise. Instead, he was just letting me know that…no matter what curve or misdirection life offers, you should live for that moment alone, and simply enjoy where you are. And that, even though his flock was way off their destination, they were happy and content because he and his friends had found a nice pond in which to soak their feet and catch a few minnows.

After all these years, it finally all made sense. The message was so simple.

As long as the path eventually leads home, it doesn't matter how long it takes to get there.

I laugh aloud and can't believe that it has taken me so much time, and the passing of a dear friend, to realize that moving thousands of miles away, and starting a new life was the only way I could find the long and winding path that led back here to this very moment and time.

I raise my face to the heavens, close my eyes, and whisper, "Thank you."

"You're welcome," comes the unexpected answer. Only it doesn't come from above.

I open my eyes, turn, and there stands my hope, my destiny, my love.

"I missed you," says my wife, Mignonne, in only the way that she can say it. A way that makes you feel like you've truly been missed.

I stand, scoop her into my arms, and squeeze her tightly, as if my very existence depends on her arms around me. I have been emotional since I heard of Jason's death, but as I hug my wife, the sense of grief and loss that have been haunting me for the longest time, comes pouring out.

We silently stand there holding each other, subtly swaying back and forth as if we're dancing to a soft melody; but there is no music, just the gentle breeze rustling through the leaves. Everything becomes calm and quiet, as if nature has brought the two of us together longing to hear our hearts as they join in one rhythmic beat of peace, harmony, and love.

I raise my head from her shoulder and gaze into those ocean blue eyes that I fell in love with so long ago.

"I missed you too," I say with a smile. "How did you know where I was?"

"I was the girl Pat was having tea with when he called you. He knew where you were."

"I'm so glad you came." A thought occurs to me. "Where are the kids and what about your classes?"

She places a finger on my lips to shush me. "The kids are with friends, and my classes weren't more important than this. Once school and the kids were taken care of, I just hopped on a plane and came. After I landed and saw how many messages there were from you on my cell, I knew I had made the right decision. She gently kisses me. "Now, what can I do for you? How can I help?" she asks in a voice just above a sigh.

"Just keep loving me and never leave."

"Never," she promises with a shake of her head, then takes her thumb and wipes the tears from my cheek. "Can I ask what you're doing here at the old wall?"

We sit, and I tell her about all that's happened since I arrived, everyone I've seen, and the information I've been given. Then I show her Jason's papers and the picture. It's her time to cry now, and I take her in my arms again.

After a while she pulls away.

"Who were you thanking when I walked up?" she asks tearfully.

I shake my head, not sure how to answer that. "God, I guess...for all that he does and has done in my life, and...also, Jason...for reminding me..."

She gives me her smile that says she doesn't really understand. "Reminding you of what?"

"Of who I really am." I take a deep breath and nervously explain my revelation, about Jason, the flamingoes, and I also include that I've been thinking that I might want to move back to Tennessee.

She remains quiet, letting me finish before she responds. Then, she throws her arms back around me.

"I am so happy to hear you say that," she says.

"Really?" I answer with surprise.

"Yes," she nods. "I've thought about moving back for quite some time, but we've been so happy in Hawaii…"

"I know, but perhaps it's time for a change, another adventure so to speak…and you won't believe this, but…" I tell her about my old house being for sale.

"Let's do it, Scott. Right now."

I grab her hand and off we go…running through the yards of my youth, and for a brief moment, time reverses. Once again, I am a child, racing home through the neighborhood of my youth and then with a big loud hop, Mignonne and I bound onto my old front porch. We ring the doorbell and kiss, giggling just as we did on this very spot so many years ago.

Sara Vaughn answers the door, surprised and smiling at the sight of us. I introduce her to Mignonne and tell her what's happened. She's ecstatic and pulls Mignonne into the house to give her the tour.

Sara is a beautiful young woman with a wonderfully large smile that grows even larger when I make her a cash offer. Overwhelmed but excited, she calls her husband and we agree to have our real estate people contact each other with details. We hug Sara and again I promise an autographed copy of my next book and one of Mignonne's as well.

We take a few more pictures of the house on the cell phone for the boys, then head back down the street to Henry's market to get my car. Mignonne pops into the store to see Mr. Henry and promises we will become regular customers again once we've moved. The news thrills him and he loads a bag full of candy for us to take home to the kids.

I sit in the car waiting and wondering how the children will feel about our decision to uproot them from their life and friends in Hawaii. They are still pretty young, but they have formed strong bonds and relationships. We will discuss all concerns or disappointments they may have, and I know that together as a family, we'll make the decision that's best for all of us.

My parents always included us kids in family matters, and to this day, I appreciate that. Sometimes we didn't understand the topic or magnitude of the situation, yet we always felt important because we had been a part of the discussion.

Yes, that's what we'll do. When we get home in a couple of days, we'll pack a picnic lunch, climb into the mini-van, and take the family somewhere where we can relax, talk, and decide our future.

Mignonne hops in the car, squeezes my hand, and offers a somber smile. "Are you ready?"

The happiness and excitement is fleeting as we remember where we're going.

SEVENTEEN

"This is Pat," the voice-mail says. "I'm sorry I can't get to the phone, but please leave me a message and I will get back to you as soon as possible."

"I'm getting his voice-mail," I say to Mignonne.

"He's there. Maybe he just can't get the phone," she huffs. "Try again. He *has* to know what Jason wrote to you."

Mignonne and I agreed that Pat should be told what Jason wrote, so I dial again.

"To me," she said, "Pat and Sherry were always more suited for one another."

"Hello," Pat finally answers, his voice low and somber.

"Hey, Bud. I'm swinging by to pick you up." There's silence on the other end and for a moment I think we've been cut off. "Pat?"

"About that." He clears his throat. "I've been thinking, Scott. Maybe I should just sneak in the back after the funeral begins."

"Why?"

"Why?…because of all the reasons I told you. My fight with Jason. My past with Sherry. It's all a mess. Heck, his sister, Mary, probably won't even want me there."

"That's ridiculous."

"No, it's not, Scott. She probably blames me for a lot of Jason's problems."

"Now you're just being paranoid." By this time I was pulling into his driveway. "Get your butt out here. I'm already in your driveway."

"Really? So Mignonne found you?"

"She's with me."

"All right, fine." He hangs up and in a few seconds comes around the back of the house.

Mignonne and I get out of the car.

Pat's wearing a blue suit that's a bit dated and slightly wrinkled, a red tie, and scuffed dress shoes he's probably had since college.

"You look really nice, Pat," Mig says, always finding the positive. "I like your tie."

"Thanks." He flips his tie absentmindedly. "I don't think I've worn this suit since my father's funeral. I'm afraid I'm not quite current with today's styles." He hesitates a moment and it seems he wants to say something but isn't sure how to begin.

I move closer to him. "Pat…"

"I can't believe this has happened," he interrupts. "So much…time has passed with so much sadness…and no chance to…atone…tell Jason how sorry I am or even goodbye."

Mignonne takes my arm and squeezes.

"Pat," I say. "Jason knew."

"Knew what?"

Mignonne raises her hand. In it is Jason's request.

"What's that?" he asks.

I glance at Mignonne. She nods and offers the pages to Pat. "Read this, Pat."

He pushes it away. "No." Tears flow down his cheeks.

"Pat," I urge. "Please read it."

"I can't," he whispers.

"Can I read it to you?" Mignonne asks.

It's barely discernable, but he nods.

She begins where Jason asks me to talk to Jason.

"Scott, I need you to talk to Pat for me. In the last few years, he and I…well…we had a falling out and I always regretted the things I said to him. But after a while it just seemed too late to mend the fence so I need your wisdom on this. The reason for our falling out was simple. He was in love with Sherry and deep down I knew she was in love with him too. I blew up, and still to this day I don't understand why. I knew that Sherry and I should never get married. I loved her more than anyone, but we weren't meant to be together. Our relationship was a lot like beer and wine, good to have at a party but never in the same glass."

I watch Pat's face, hoping for some sign that this is reaching him. The tears are there, but his eyes seem distant, glazed over.

Mignonne continues.

"Pat was good to and good for Sherry. He remembered things about her and always knew the right thing to say and how to make her feel good about herself. Truth is, it was actually fun watching the two of them together, laughing and picking on each other. I know that both of them are hurting now and I've been the cause of that hurt for too long."

She stops and looks up at Pat. Still no change of expression just his stoic face wet with tears. She reads the final paragraph.

"Scott, tell Pat that I'm sorry, that I love him, and that if the feelings are still there, he should tell Sherry and not waste another minute of his life without her. Tell him that if I could have one more minute with him, it would be to tell him that he is the better man and the better friend."

Mignonne finishes and we both watch Pat.

For a moment he just stares at the ground, then slowly turns away from us. "Oh, Jason," he says quietly as he raises his hands. He sobs for a moment, then falls to his knees.

We race over, kneel beside him, and take him in our arms.

"It's okay, Pat," I say, my voice breaking. "It's okay."

At that point, Pat Wilson and I cry together, and if I remember correctly, it's the first time. Sure, we've each been there for the other during sad times. But never, have we experienced this. This *shared* feeling of loss, grief, and bereavement.

Mignonne stands, places her hands on the two of us, and says a prayer.

"Dear, Lord. Please bless these two men that I love and care about so greatly. Father, give them the strength to get through this day as they say goodbye to Jason Maler. Fill their hearts with grace, love, and wonderful memories of their friend and brother." She's crying now. "And thank you, Lord, for Jason, and for giving him the wisdom to give us the gift of this letter…the gift of these words that offer forgiveness, comfort, encouragement, and love." She pauses, then takes Pat's arm, lifts him to her, and kisses his forehead. "Please, God. Come to Pat and bring Jason's forgiveness and love. Let Thy Will Be Done, Father, and show us the way best to serve thy will. Amen."

"Amen," Pat and I say in unison.

"Jinx." Pat smiles at me through tears. "You owe me a Coke."

We all laughed, then Pat hugs me and Mignonne and tells us he loves us.

"Thank you so much." he says. "For being my friends."

He lets go, takes out a handkerchief, and wipes his eyes. "So…what do you guys think Sherry will think about this?"

As if on cue…

"Hey," a soft voice says from behind us.

We turn and see Sherry standing there. I don't think I've ever seen her look more beautiful. She's wearing a simple black dress, low heeled shoes and no make-up. Her hair is curled and cascades over her shoulders in loose auburn ringlets. She's biting her lip and seems a bit nervous, and like the rest of us, there are tears in her eyes.

"Hey, Sherry," Pat gasps. "You look beautiful."

"Thanks," she responds quietly, then lowers her head and takes a deep breath as if gathering her courage. "Pat?" She raises her head and walks forward. "I need to talk to you."

Just then, Mignonne and I notice the manilla envelope in *her* hand.

EIGHTEEN

The funeral home parking lot is jam packed with cars, trucks, and SUVs, on both levels of the lot, and many more in the grass. A smile comes, and I know that all of these people are here for Jason. No, not because I'm psychic or anything silly like that. I know it because in the past couple of days, I've seen how many people's lives have been touched by Jason Maler. The sight makes me both happy and sad. Happy because so many cared about him, sad because he isn't here to see how greatly he was loved and how badly he will be missed. However, if you believe the way I do, then you realize in your heart that somehow...Jason will know.

It's just me and Mignonne in the car. Pat and Sherry decided to ride together in Pat's car. Understandable, really. After all, Jason had left Sherry a letter as well. A letter that said basically the same things that Jason's letter had said to me: That he was sorry for all of the pain and sorrow he had caused Sherry and that he would hold her love in his heart and soul as long as God permitted. Then he told her that she should be happy and not waste any time mourning for him. He wanted her to start living the life he knew she deserved, with the person she wanted to share it with. He then added: *If that person is Pat you both have my blessing.*

After reading it, Pat he took Sherry in his arms and gave her the kiss I knew he had been saving for years. A wonderfully warm sense of joy and fulfillment swept over me and at that very moment I felt it. I knew...everything was going to be all right.

Searching for a parking spot, I pull around the back of the funeral home and see Bob Shears, the funeral director, waving at me.

"Hey, Mr. Shears," I say after rolling down my window.

"Hey, Scott," he says as he offers his hand through the window. "It's good to see you, friend."

"Thanks."

"Listen, Scott. Jason's sister Mary wants to see you as soon as you get in. She's in my office."

"Okay," I reply. I haven't seen Mary Maler Pierce in years. She was born when Jason was ten and at first he was a bit resentful but as the two of them got older he came to adore her. Sometimes he was a bit overprotective, but she was a feisty little girl and would put her big brother in his place pretty quickly.

Pat told me a while back that Jason and Mary's relationship changed when Mary announced she was getting married to Tom Pierce. Tom was a real estate investor with, what Jason thought, was a somewhat questionable past and Jason was afraid that Mary would end up hurt or destitute.

However, Tom had cleared his name. Turns out, Tom had met this guy at a realtors' seminar and partnered with him on a subdivision deal with little investment on Tom's part. Six months later, Tom had been approached by the T.B.I. and was told his partner was a crook and wanted for questioning in Mexico and the Bahamas. Tom was shocked and agreed to do whatever to clear his own name and had gone undercover to get proof of any criminal activity. In the end, the guy was arrested and all Tom was guilty of was stupidity. Mary and Tom then moved to Kentucky to start over and had been there ever since. Hopefully, she and Jason had resolved things.

We finally find a parking space in the employee lot beside Mr. Shears truck, then enter the funeral through the back door and I make a bee line for Mr. Shears office. A few people notice me and call my name. I give a slight wave and send Mignonne over to them to explain to them that I have to take care of something before I can visit.

I reach Mr. Shears office, knock on the door, and barely hear a faint reply.

"Come in."

I open the door a bit and poke my head in. "Mary?"

"Oh, Scott." Sitting on the loveseat in Mr. Shears office is Mary Pierce. She puts down a cup of coffee and comes over as I enter. "I'm so glad you're here."

Mary Pierce is still as cute as she was at twelve years old. She's petite, about five feet one inches tall, and has probably never weighed more than a hundred pounds. She hugs me tightly, pressing her head against my chest.

We stand there for awhile, not able to speak, just holding each other, crying and breathing. Her heart beat is strong against my chest and feels in rhythm with my own. For a fleeting moment I feel as if Jason is in the room with us.

"Mary?" I say.

She doesn't answer but I know she's listening.

"When was the last time you spoke with Jason?"

She squeezes me tightly, then answers. "He called about two weeks ago and said that he was sending me something. I asked him what it was but he wouldn't tell me anything other than it was some papers. Then we just talked for a while, not about anything in particular, just talked, like we used to when we were younger. It was really nice."

I release her and motion for her to sit. She retrieves her coffee cup from the end table and sits beside me on the small office sofa.

"Mary, did you know Jason was sick?"

"Yes," she says with a nod. "Or at least I knew it the first time. I thought he was still in remission. I didn't know it had come back until Sherry called about the wreck and told me everything the doctor had told her." She starts to tear up again, so I hand her my handkerchief. This time I had wisely brought two. "Did you know he was sick, Scott?"

"Not until a couple of days ago." I stand, again feeling guilt and regret. "I hadn't spoken to him in a while."

"Any particular reason?" she asks. "I know he and Pat had had a falling out."

"No," I answer. "Just too wrapped up in my own life I guess. Taking for granted that friends and family will always be there."

"Don't do that to yourself, Scott. Jason loved you like a brother. I never heard him say a negative thing about you, or Pat for that matter."

Remembering, I turn to her. "The papers Jason called about and sent you...can I ask what they were?"

"There was a brief note attached to a thick envelope. It said he had met with his lawyer and had his will drafted. No info on the contents, just that the package wasn't to be opened until his death. It also said that if I died before he did, the papers were to go to my estate for my children to open." She shakes her head. "He said it wasn't any big deal, just wanted to get some things settled. I didn't think much about it, just figured his cancer made him grow up and get responsible. That's a natural reaction, isn't it."

"I would think so, yes." I walk over and sit down again. "Mary, have you opened the package he sent you?"

"Yes."

"And...?"

"It was another note, attached to a million dollar life insurance policy. Scott, he took the policy out when he was twenty-five and named me the beneficiary." She wipes her eyes. "The note said that he figured with his lifestyle back then, if something unexpected happened to him he wanted me to be okay."

I reach over and take her hand. "He loved you very much, Mary."

"I know," she says. "He also left me most of his unsold paintings."

"Most?" I smile, thinking that is typical Jason.

"All but one, actually."

"Which one? Did he give a reason?"

She answers no with a shake of her head.

"Mary, what about your parents' old farm?"

"He had plans for that".

"What plans?"

"I can't say right now."

I stand, and from my pocket I pull the papers Jason left me. "Mary, he left me a note as well."

"I know."

I nod. "Would you like to read it?"

"Sure." She takes the letter from me and begins reading.

There's a gentle knock at the door followed by Bob Shears "Excuse me, but people are asking for you guys."

"Okay, Mr. Shears," I answer. "We'll be out in a minute."

"Fine." He leaves us alone again.

I turn back to Mary and see the tears rolling down her cheeks, staining the pages her brother has written. A few minutes later, she folds the letter and hands it back to me.

"Oh, Scott," she says with a sigh. "Have you talked to Sherry or Pat yet?"

I tell her all that has happened with Pat and Sherry in the last hour and she seems genuinely happy for them.

She stands, reaches out for my hand, then we embrace. "Scott, I know this is short notice. But would you speak today?"

"Speak?" I stammer.

"You know Jason wasn't really religious. He was more of a spiritual person, a free spirit, so I don't think a minister who never knew him will be able to say the right things."

I know she's right, but have doubts about my ability to say the right things either.

"Please, Scott."

"Okay," I find myself saying.

She hugs me once more, then turns towards the door.

We exit and find Mignonne, Pat and Sherry all standing outside Mr. Shears office, waiting for us to join them before entering the chapel. Mary takes both Pat and Sherry into her arms and tells them she loves them. Mignonne and I watch the three of them huddled together and I realize something. Because of the sad circumstance that brings us here today, three lives are now beginning to heal.

I take Mignonne's hand and walk away feeling that this is a private moment that Pat, Sherry, and Mary need to share with each other.

"Hey?" Mignonne says. "You all right?"

I think about that one for a while, wondering what reply will best answer her question. She senses this and squeezes my hand.

"Let me just say that...I believe everything is going to be all right, myself included."

She offers me one of her glorious smiles, the kind that made me fall in love with her.

"Mary has asked me to speak, give a eulogy of sorts."

"You can do that," she says.

I appreciate her confidence in me, but truth be told, she is the better speaker; and as much as I hate to admit it, the better writer. Sure, I can be entertaining and get a point across to a bunch of fiction readers, but that isn't what is needed here today. I feel Jason and Mary and all of the people who have come to pay their last respects deserve better.

After all, over the past few years, they seemed to know Jason better than I did. So shouldn't they expect a wonderful eulogy given by someone more thoughtful and caring than myself? Someone who hasn't been so self-centered and absorbed with his own life that he let his relationship with one of his best friends deteriorate and wither away?

I think so, but apparently Mary Maler Pierce thinks otherwise.

"Scott?"

"Yes." I raise my eyes and see in Mignonne's eyes the love that she has for me and the love she knows I have for Jason.

She places her hand over my heart and my pulse quickens. "It's all in there. Just say it."

NINETEEN

Mignonne and I are overwhelmed at the number of people occupying the chapel. We greet as many as we can before the funeral director asks us to take our seats. The minister says a few words, offers a prayer, then introduces me.

It may not happen to everyone, but when I stand alone in front of a large group of people I get nervous. Oh, I've done it many times, but it's something I've never gotten comfortable doing. My secret to public speaking is simple. I search for a friendly face in the crowd, not always someone I know, but someone who just has that pleasant type of face. You know the one, warm, smiling, appreciative of you being up there front and center.

I've had no time to prepare, so I just lay the papers Jason left me on the podium, clear my throat, and raise my head. I begin searching for that friendly face and don't see a single one. Instead, I see about three hundred. It's a full house, standing room only, and the crowd seems to flow out into the lobby as well.

How I wish Jason was here to see this, to feel the love in this room. So many times in our youth, Jason had felt alone, friendless. Now, here were hundreds of people from all walks of life scattered throughout this audience. People who knew, respected, and loved Jason Maler. People whose lives were changed for the better because they knew him and people whose lives wouldn't be the same with him gone.

I see Mignonne, Pat, Sherry and Mary of course. But I also see Nancy Law, Laura Anderson, Clarence and Mona Jackson. There are other familiar faces as well. Lucinda Williams is standing near the back of the room, along with several of our old high school classmates. A couple of our high school teachers are in the fifth row and I recognize one of them as the art teacher.

I'm still a bit nervous, not sure what to say, but for the most part, I feel that no matter what *I* say, everyone will have their own story about Jason Maler. Comforted by that thought, I take a deep breath and start.

"Hey, everybody," I say. "I would like to begin today by offering a few apologies. First, for how long this may take since I am sure I'm going to get emotional and secondly, for not being adequately prepared and," I hold up the letter, "third for using someone else's material. You'll understand that statement in a minute." I lay the papers back down. "And finally, I apologize for being away for so long and for not keeping in contact with Jason, Pat, and with so many of you. Many of the best times in my life were spent with the people in this very room." I swallow hard, trying to choke back my emotions. "I have been remiss and negligent in telling you that and I want you to know how much I care for and miss each of you and…" I can't hold it back anymore. The tears come and my voice breaks, "I hope that you will forgive me and give me the chance to redeem that failure."

I fold my hands on the podium, lower my head and cry, feeling powerless over the emotions that gush forth. I pray silently for God to help me get through this and he answers quickly. Pat, Sherry, Nancy Law and Laura Anderson, Clarence Jackson and Ms. Mona, all come forward and lay their hands upon me and whisper words of encouragement and prayer. It's an amazing feeling, having all the love and forgiveness of each of them passing into my heart, giving me the strength to continue. I hug each of them, thank them, and tell them that I think I'm okay to continue now so they can sit back down.

I grab my handkerchief and wipe my eyes knowing it's pointless, but it at least slackens the stream a bit. I look up and Mignonne blows me a kiss, then I continue.

"When Mignonne and I entered the chapel, we were surprised and so very pleased at the number of visitors here today. There are many that we know and haven't seen for years, and there are others we are meeting for the first time and hopefully not the last. It has been so wonderful talking to each of you and hearing all of the wonderful stories and memories you have of Jason. Thank you so much, and bless you all for these and for all of the smiles and tears, and simply for being here and sharing all of the things a life, or rather the passing of a life, should have.

Thank you also to Clarence Jackson and Ms. Mona for bringing this wonderful food and for making sure everyone has coffee or tea, and for taking care of so many of us for so many years. Thank you to all of the people I have met today who told me they were clients of Jason's, and for sharing stories about how he had remodeled, landscaped or painted for them. You guys knew a different Jason than I did, and it means so much to me to know about that part of his life.

But most of all, I am so moved by how many of our former classmates are here. For all those high school years, Jason thought he didn't fit in, wasn't liked, and didn't have any real friends besides Pat, Sherry, Mignonne, and myself. Oh, how wrong he was. Maybe some or even most of these friendships and acquaintances have come after high school but that doesn't matter. The fact that all of you came..." I extend my arms towards the crowd. "This here is proof, sitting and standing before me, that Jason Maler had friends, had family, had respect, and most of all had love." The tears come again but gently this time, not a torrent. "And I dearly hope at the end…he had peace…and most of all happiness."

Once again, I dab at my eyes and cheeks. "The last thing Jason would have wanted to listen to was a bunch of my weepy ramblings. So I have decided to use his words and share something that he wanted me to do something with. Something he thought was important." I grip the pages. "Jason left me a letter and package and this is what he wrote to me."

> *"A few years ago, I found this in my closet. I had forgotten so much of this, but when I reread it…that moment in my life, our lives, came flooding back, and the memories of that experience are what have guided me through these final years. The serenity and peace of that day and those beautiful creatures have brought balance into my life and taught me the most valuable lesson of my life. Do you remember this quote?*
>
> *"Could it be, that even though he was way off his destination, he was happy and content because he and his friends had found a nice pond in which to soak their feet and catch a few minnows, and that as long as the path eventually led home, it didn't matter how long it took to get there?"*

I lay the pages down and clear my throat again. "Jason was referring to the summer of nineteen-seventy-eight and a wonderful experience that occurred during that summer. The quote was from a short story I wrote in nineteen-seventy-eight about that experience. I gave Jason that story, and apparently *that* summer combined with my story had quite an affect on Jason and he thought it was important for me to remember that time and to have the story back. I won't prolong this service by reading it, but if any of you want to read it, let me know and I'll get you a copy.

At that moment, Mary Maler Pierce, stands. "I'd like to hear it."

Mignonne was sitting beside Mary and stand as well. "Me too." One by one everyone in the chapel stands and asks to hear the story that had meant so much to Jason.

And so I begin...

"The Summer of the Pink Flamingoes by J. Scott Sawyer."

TWENTY

It's an incredible feeling...to have so many people's attention, and know that they are all listening intently to what you have to say. During my story, there are smiles and sighs, several moments of out loud laughter and many, many tears. When I finish, there's a brief moment of silence followed by applause. I glance upwards, close my eyes, and send my love to Jason.

The minister comes up, shakes my hand, and thanks me for my wonderful words. He then takes the podium and makes an announcement.

"Jason requested cremation..." He points to the urn before the podium. "With the details of his internment to be announced later to a family member, namely, his sister, Mary. There will be no grave-side service and this is to be the only memorial as per Jason's instructions, so if anyone has something they would like to share, now is the time." He sits and Nancy Law is the first to speak.

She is very honest, admitting her admiration, friendship, and love for Jason. Laura Anderson talks about our high school adventures and a few other classmates join in. When they finish, Sherry Masters stands nervously before the microphone and tells the memorable story of a high school crush that led to a long-time relationship filled with many highs and lows, emotions and twists, pain and sorrow, but mostly filled with love. After she finishes, the sanctuary is very quiet. The minister glances around with raised eyebrows, silently asking if there is anyone else, and that's when Pat Wilson stands and takes the podium. He has difficulty expressing himself at first but eventually finds the words.

"As most of you know, Scott, Jason, and I have been friends for more than twenty-seven years. Our relationship began when we were fifteen, has continued up until this moment, and hopefully, will continue throughout eternity. We have always cared for and been there for one another...however, there have been many trials of loyalty and tests of faith within our bonds of friendship. It's difficult and sad to say...but there have been times when we were angry with one another, one of us wasn't speaking to the other, or one of us went away and didn't keep in touch, or a time when *one* of us...betrayed the other's trust..." At this point he breaks down and Sherry goes to him. She takes him in her arms and holds him for a moment. Then he seems to regain his composure, lets go of her, and continues.

"Many of you know me and...well, you know that I haven't always been the most successful person," he laughs softly, "at business or romance." He glances over at Sherry and she squeezes his hand. "But during these past couple of days, I discovered that I *have* been successful at something...a true friendship."

"Oh, Pat," Sherry sighs.

"Scott and I always thought that *we* took Jason under our wing and gave him the privilege of our friendship and guidance and, well...that may have been how it started...but in the end...as you can plainly see...it was clearly Jason that held us together all along and brought us all together here today." Pat's voice drops to a whisper. "He's given all of us a gift, people. A gift of inspiration, hope, and faith in one another. But to me…he's given what I think is the greatest gift of all…his forgiveness…and his blessing." He turns to Sherry, kisses her, and I think I can read his lips well enough to see him say, *I Love You.* They cry together for a moment then make their way back to their seats leaving one final person to speak.

Mary Pierce is petite and quiet, a stark contrast to her big brother, but I always felt she was the stronger of the two. She became the only woman in the house at the age of four when her mother died, took charge of all arrangements when their father passed, and now has to be the head of the family once more and put her brother to rest.

She coughs nervously, squeezes the handkerchief I gave her and begins. "Thank you all so much for coming. I am a good bit younger than Jason and moved away quite a while back, so I don't know all of you, but I it means so much to me to hear wonderful things about my brother and how much he meant to so many of you. I came here today…as the final member of our family…to take care of my brother…but as he has done so many times before, he has taken care of me. You all have told so many wonderful stories and memories that I feel that all there is left to say is…goodbye."

Her husband, Tom, is waiting at the base of the podium. She steps down, takes Jason's urn and the two of them walk down the aisle. Softly in the background, Dan Fogelberg's beautiful ballad, *To The Morning,* begins to play and at that moment, we all stand, join hands and say goodbye to Jason Maler.

There are at least a hundred floral arrangements around the hand-carved oak stand upon which his urn rested. Technically, I guess they aren't floral arrangements but live plants. As we leave the chapel, I notice the plants aren't being moved. I question Mr. Shears about this, wondering what's to become of all of these plants. He gives my arm a gentle squeeze and assures me everything is taken care of.

As we leave the funeral home and say our last goodbyes to the many people who have suddenly resurfaced in my life, I am filled with sadness and joy. It's sad to have lost Jason and to be parting from his many friends, but joyful to have had the opportunity to reunite with so many people from my past. The last hand I shake is Clarence Jackson's.

"I can't tell you what a pleasure it's been to have you and Mignonne back in town"

"Thanks, Clarence." I reply. "You and Ms. Mona have been so wonderful to all of us over the past few days and that has meant so much."

I see tears forming in the corners of his eyes and I feel my own eyes getting a bit wet. He hugs me and about beats me to death, but it's loving and warm and means the world to me. He releases me and takes Mignonne gently in his arms.

"Come back soon, pretty lady. I want to see those boys."

"Sooner than you can imagine," Mignonne says with genuine promise.

I put my arm around Mig and we wave to the last remnant of people rambling through the parking lot. Yes, it has been a funeral...touching upon grief, remorse, and a bit of regret, but it has also been a reunion of sorts, filled with hope, promise, and love. I think Jason would have been pleased that he got everyone together again, even if just for a brief moment of time.

We turn towards the car and see Lucinda leaning against the BMW.

"Hey, Luce," I say with a sniffle."

She's crying too.

"Beautiful eulogy, Scott."

"Thanks." I introduce her and Mignonne and they exchange hugs.

She wipes a tear away. "So when do you guys fly out?"

"Ten o'clock." I glance at my watch. "Five hours from now."

She smiles. "Then there's time."

"Time for what?"

She pulls another a manilla folder from her purse and hands it to me. "This is the last one…one final thing that Jason wanted me to give you."

I take it. "Can I open it?"

"You have to," she says with a nod. "Otherwise you won't know what you're supposed to do."

I gently tear the seal and pull out a standard sized piece of white writing paper. On it is Jason's handwriting.

"It's directions with a map sketched on the bottom of the page." I raise my eyes and see Lucinda walking towards her car. "Lucinda. What is this?"

"It's yours, Scott." She stops and turns. "He loved you very much and I can give it to you now because it's not considered part of the estate. Jason put it in your name as soon as he found out he was sick." She turns away again.

"Lucinda!"

"Just go!" she calls over her shoulder.

Mignonne takes the paper from me. "Do you know where this is?"

I close my eyes and nod. "Yes."

TWENTY-ONE

The drive is simply beautiful. Many of the Tennessee wildflowers and trees are in bloom along the winding country road that leads towards the farm Jason's parents bought when we were teenagers. It was such a wonderful place, one hundred acres of fields, woods, streams, with two huge ponds and the river running nearby. The Maler's had built a small cabin and two large barns, one for animals and another for storage.

During high school, we came out here all the time, and had parties about every other weekend. As long as we were responsible, Mr. Maler had told us we could use the place and use it we had. I probably still had a key to the cabin in my drawer at home. They had sold the place the Christmas after graduation, breaking our hearts. But they had needed the money because their savings had been depleted from four years of paying off Mrs. Maler's medical expenses.

We travel the miles from town in silence.

Mignonne has sensed that I needed this time of quiet but finally she speaks. "Okay. Where are we going?"

"The directions lead to the Maler's farm."

"The old one with the cabin? I thought they sold that."

"They did…summer after graduation."

"When Jason and Mary's mom got sick."

"Right."

Mignonne smiles. "I found some of those pictures before I left. The boys wanted to know who Jason was, so I showed them all of the ones with you, Jason, and Pat at the farm."

I choke up at the memory.

The sun is bright in the afternoon sky as we reach the turn off the main road. I stop on the shoulder and double check the map. It's been twenty-seven years since I've been here and it seems not much has changed, but I want to be sure.

"If I remember correctly, the driveway should be a mile or so down this road."

Mignonne looks around. "None of this looks familiar to me."

"Well, you hadn't been at Franklin High very long before they sold it. I think you came out, what, two or three times."

"That's probably right." Mignonne looks at the map again. "Let's venture on."

I put the car in drive and proceed. "I really expected all of this land to be developed by now. I thought Jason told me that some contractor bought the farm from his parents."

"Hey," Mignonne says. "What are these numbers at the bottom of the page?"

"What numbers?" I stop again.

"Right under the map." she points. "Look, 1845. Is that the house number?"

"No. That was the last four digits of *my* parents phone number."

"Drive, Scott."

There's a look of excitement in her eyes and I'll admit there is a great amount of curiosity on my part. I slow down as I see a familiar landmark, a giant magnolia tree that stands near the

Maler's mailbox.

"I think this is it." But as I pass the magnolia and pull into the concrete driveway, I think maybe I'm wrong. This couldn't be the Maler farm. Their driveway wasn't concrete and they definitely didn't have this large stone gate. As I study further, I notice the stone wall attached to the gate goes on and on, seemingly surrounding the property. "Maybe there were two giant magnolias on this road."

"Why do you say that?" Mignonne asks.

"Because the Maler's place definitely didn't have an entrance like this. Most of the time, their mailbox was leaning against the magnolia tree because some kids had knocked it over with a bat or beer bottle." I glance at Mignonne and her mouth is hanging open.

"What," I ask.

"Look," she says, pointing at the gate.

"Oh, my gosh."

She nods and turns to me. "You don't think."

"I don't know," I reply.

"Try it and see," she prods.

"Okay." I roll down my window and punch 1845 into the keypad. There is a moment of silence then the creaking wooden gates of *Flamingo Hall* slowly open and again I remember the words...

I had misunderstood the flamingo. He wasn't inviting me to come with him to his tropical paradise. Maybe, just maybe, he was telling me that no matter what curve or misdirection life throws you, that you should live for the moment, and enjoy where you are. Even though he was way off his destination, he was happy and content because he and his friends had found a nice pond in which to soak their feet, and catch a few minnows, and that as long as the path eventually led home, it didn't matter how long it took to get there?

We pull through the gate and are greeted by a thick grove of trees, the woods I recall from my youth. I glance in the rear-view mirror and see the gate begin to close. The concrete goes forward into the woods, a seemingly endless path that grows darker as we enter the forest. Through the sunroof, I see brief glints of sunlight piercing the thick canopy of limbs and leaves above. Beautiful.

"Scott, stop," Mignonne shouts.

I look ahead just in time to brake for eight deer crossing. After waiting a couple of minutes for any stragglers, we continue and come to a covered bridge with open sides.

"That's definitely new," I say. "The water here was never very deep and the driveway used to have a low natural bridge lined with railroad ties and brick."

"It looks like the woods open after you cross the bridge."

We cross the bridge slowly and glance down at the rushing stream below.

"Is that the Harpeth River?" Mignonne asks.

"No, it's just a small creek. I never heard a name if it had one."

We exit the bridge, drive another quarter mile, and I slam on the brakes.

"Oh my gosh," we both say at the same time.

Before us is a valley of beauty, color, and splendor. Fruit trees and shrubs are ablaze along the edges of the driveway with flowers landscaped in circles around each tree and bush. There are fountains and waterways edging each flower bed and leading along the walking paths towards where the cabin used to be and, I assume, the five acre pond behind it.

In the cabin's place now stands an enormous chalet made entirely of logs and decking, all covered with a gleaming silver metal roof.

We take the circular driveway up to the house and park, thinking someone will see or hear us and come out to greet us, but it doesn't happen. Mignonne and I exchange glances, shrug our shoulders, and exit the car. A gentle breeze wafts over us and it's hard to describe the air at that moment. There is definitely the scent of jasmine, cedar, and roses, and just a hint of lavender...

SQUAWK

"What was that?" I can't really tell if it came from the woods or from behind the house

"Oh, good, you heard it too." Mignonne says.

"Odd?" I say.

"What?"

"Something...familiar."

She sighs. "So, what now?"

I take her hand and up the stairs we go, onto one of the most beautiful wrap around porches I have ever seen. The wood is cedar, wide planks with a clear stain, and each totem-pole-style support post is uniquely carved with images of a different animal or bird. I can't imagine how many painstaking hours it must have taken to do this. There's a post with a bear, a moose, a wolf, a trout, an eagle...I sense it before I actually see it, but there it is. I walk over and delicately rub my hand over the column that holds the face of the bird I know so well.

"Jason did this," I whisper.

"Hey," Mignonne calls from behind.

I turn and see her standing in the doorway. "It's unlocked."

The door itself is the work of a master craftsman, with etched glass, mahogany trim, and iron fixtures. Again probably Jason. I step inside and realize the door is rather plain compared to the room before me. It's massive, maybe a thousand square feet. Oversized picture windows adorn the front and right walls with oak bookcases in between. The ceiling is at least fifteen feet high with thick exposed burnished beams and a very large elk antler chandelier.

An enormous stone fireplace occupies the center of the room

like a sculpture. It is openly vented on all sides, has wrought iron corner columns, and is approximately eight feet square with a seating area surrounding it. Comfortable, overstuffed, leather chairs, love-seats, and ottomans, with small tables placed strategically between, enclose the hearth like a campfire circle.

A winding wooden staircase ascends behind the fireplace.

"This is the coolest room I've ever been in," I say.

On the left wall of this great room are three solid wood doors. Our curiosity is peaked, so we enter them all.

The first room is fairly large, about twenty by twenty, and the walls here are also lined with bookshelves in between the picture windows. Near one of these windows is a massive hand made cherry desk with a computer and a flat screen monitor on it. Tucked in the corner of the room, under one of the large windows, is a well worn leather sofa that appears to have been used for naps because there is a long indention across the cushions. An indention about the size of Jason.

"This was his office," I say.

"Hey," Mignonne says. "Look at this." She's standing in front of the sofa looking at the pictures above it.

I move closer and the tears come again. Before us are at least a hundred framed photographs of Jason, Mary, his parents, Pat, Sherry, Mignonne, myself, and many others, that range in age from early childhood to the present. Most are beautifully captured in black and white but a few of the sunrises and sunset photos are in color. Several of the pictures are of the posed variety, like the school photos of my kids we send each year, a couple of graduation head-shots, and a few wedding pictures. But most of the pictures were candidly taken at the farm parties, during trips, or just around town. There are also some great landscape shots of the farm during the four seasons, but the picture I'm looking for is the one taken during the summer of

1978. It isn't here on the wall. Had he given me the only copy?

Mignonne, sensing I need time alone with these memories, moves to the next room. I follow shortly and find her at the middle door, a half bath that looks out into the woods. Paintings line these walls, mostly nature scenes of fall leaves and snow flocked trees. Jason's initials are painted in the bottom corner of each one.

The third and final door on this wall is a music room. A full sized drum set occupies the far corner, and a variety of guitars, both electric and acoustic, are scattered about the room. A variety of amplifiers and speakers hang from the ceiling, just like in a studio. One wall is covered with shelves that are piled with stacks of CD's, vinyl albums and cassette tapes. The other walls are covered with posters and concert hand-bills, all displaying bands and concerts that were favorites of ours back in high school. Zeppelin, AC/DC, Journey, Kiss, ELO, and many more are here. Yes, there is even an autographed Village People poster. Some of the bands I don't recognize, but I figure they're more current bands who Jason liked.

I walk over and search the CD's, which are arranged alphabetically, and find a few of the newer bands' CD's and make a mental note to borrow one before I leave. I'll give it a listen, and maybe get a little bit better understanding of Jason's music tastes in his later years.

Mignonne exits the room, leaving me with my thoughts.

"Scott," she calls. "You'll want to see this."

Curious, I go to see what she's found, and my attention is immediately drawn to the mantle, actually above it. He has captured, so beautifully, the picture I have come to cherish so much. The pastel mural is in three side-by-side sections, each panel measuring four feet square. Jason is in the left panel and I'm in the right, our arms raised as the flamingoes take flight across all three sections. An eight by ten photo, just like the smaller version

I have, is propped on the mantle beneath.

I close my eyes, and for a moment I am taken back and feel the gush of wind caused by their flapping wings.

I feel Mignonne's arm around me and open my eyes.

"It's amazing, Scott."

She's right. I am overwhelmed and highly emotional, knowing that this image will be a part of my soul for the rest of my life.

"Mary said that Jason left her all but one of his unsold paintings," I say. "This must be it."

"I wonder why?" Mignonne asks.

"With Jason, there didn't always have to be a reason." I suddenly realize that Mignonne is holding a white envelope and my name is on it. "What's that?"

"I have no clue," she answers. "It was on the mantle beside the picture.

I take it and see it's not sealed, so I pull the flap loose and remove another sheet of plain white paper adorned with Jason's handwriting. Through the tears, I can barely make out the words.

Scott,

> *I know this has been an emotional day for you but I hope to finish it with a happy ending. I hope you are impressed with the house and the farm. Actually, I hope you love it…because it is now yours. Most of the best memories I have…were the times I spent with you, Pat, Sherry, and my family on this farm. After I discovered I was sick, I decided to build the shop, renovate the house, and make some changes to the pond, because I wanted to be inspired and relive some of fondest memories. You'll see what I'm talking about in a minute.*

> *I know you're probably overwhelmed and thinking you can't accept this, but you have to, because it's already been*

done. Lucinda has the deed and it's in your name, buddy. I asked Mary about this before making a final decision, and she thought it was a great idea that you and your family have the place. She doesn't want to move back to Tennessee, and was glad the friend we most considered family would now be the owner.

I have no clue whether you, Mignonne, and the boys will want to move back to Tennessee either, but hope, if not, you will come up with a plan for the place. I trust your judgment and know you will make the right decision. Whatever you decide, let Lucinda know and she'll take care of it.

I wish I could be there when you go out back.

Love always,
Jason

I glance up and Mignonne is gone. Then I hear the creaking of stairs and see her coming down the steps.

"There's five bedrooms and four full baths up there," she says.

"Read this."

She takes the page and reads it. "Oh my."

"I know."

We then take each other's hand and walk through arched French doors to a glorious kitchen. It's a chef's dream with a Viking stove, stainless steel prep racks, two dishwashers, and an abundance of cabinet and counter space.

"Why would Jason need such a big, well-equipped kitchen?" Mignonne asks.

"I don't know," I answer with a shrug. "Maybe he entertained a lot."

Another set of French doors line the rear kitchen wall and lead outside to the wrap-around porch. Not sure what to expect, we open the door, walk outside, and we both gasp at the same time. Beyond the porch is the five acre pond I remember so well, but it had never looked like this.

A ten foot waterfall cascades from the hillside, splashing leisurely into the huge pond, causing peaceful ripples across the water. Fifty foot willow trees surround the liquid mirror that is now reflecting the cloudless azure sky. Honeybees buzz around hundreds of varieties of wildflowers that grow to the edge of the pond and seem to trail right into the water, and I see several fish, bass or perch probably, lazily wiggling their tails near the shallows.

A tributary branches off of the pond and treks across the grassy field, disappearing into the woods near the creek.

I'm impressed. "I guess Jason had dug that out to give the pond some flow and so it would catch floodwater from the creek."

"Was the pond house always there?" Mignonne asks, pointing towards a grey stone-covered, pink trimmed, cottage that sits near the waterfall. It's good sized, maybe thirty feet square.

"I don't remember a pond house."

"I wonder if that's Jason's wood shop or art studio."

I glance to the right and see a rather large barn-like structure with a wood stove chimney and vent system coming out of the roof.

"I don't think so. That building over there looks to be set up for a shop. It's got an exhaust system and has really big doors."

SQUAWK

There's that noise again.

Mignonne and I both spin our heads around and our mouths drop open wide when we see the glorious creature emerge from the cottage.

"I don't believe it," I gasp.

Out comes another, then another, and one more. It's a parade, or rather...a flock. The first flamingo has now been joined by at least a dozen of his pink fuzzy friends. At first, I feel dazed and lightheaded as if awakening from a dream, and even reach for the porch rail to steady myself as I watch the flamingoes flap their wings, squawk, and slowly strut from their house to the cool, rippling water. Not at all fazed by our presence, they act as if they've lived here their entire lives...and I wonder if they have.

I glance at Mignonne and see tears. Her eyes meet mine and she looks as if she wants to speak but can't find the words. I know exactly how she feels. We return our attention to the beautiful birds, and at that moment, I feel an emotion that can only be described with one word.

"Heaven."

TWENTY-TWO

One year later...

My favorite time of day has always been sunset, and living in Hawaii, I've seen some glorious ones. However, the sunsets I have always found the most beautiful, are the summertime sunsets in Tennessee. I know some people disagree, and they are entitled to their opinion, but no one will ever convince me otherwise. Probably because my family spent so many summer evenings on the porch watching the sun say goodnight, or maybe because I told my wife I loved her for the first time during one of those sunsets. Who knows?

What I do know, is that I have never seen a sky as beautiful as the one before me now. There are so many glorious tints and patterns up in the heavens...that I feel God is up there right now working with a paintbrush and palette full of color...and I wonder what this sunset looks like from His side.

"Hey, Dad," comes from below.

I look down and see Clay, Cameron, and a couple of other kids feeding the flamingoes. The smaller children are a bit timid around the tall, leggy birds, but Clay and Cameron have formed a loving relationship with the beautiful creatures. This bond is confirmed by the way Cameron strokes the fuzzy head of one bird and the way another one pokes his head under Clay's arm, prodding for his attention and bread crumbs.

"Hey, guys," I wave. The boys have made me so proud this past year with the way they have happily accepted and adapted to the vast changes in our lives. "Try not to get your clothes dirty just yet."

"Okay."

Last summer, as soon as school ended for Mignonne and the boys, we made the move back to Franklin, back to the old neighborhood, back to the house I grew up in. Jason made a wonderful gesture, leaving me the farm, but I just couldn't see myself living there. That was his life. Those were his memories.

Instead, I wanted to make my own *new* memories, with my family, in my former home. That may not make sense to some people, and it may sound a bit selfish, but Mignonne understands.

Besides, we had other plans for the farm.

Through Lucinda, we set up the Jason Maler Art Foundation. Through that foundation, we have turned the farm into a creative art school and retreat estate, open to children of all ages and adults who still *think* of themselves as children and desire a place where they can live out a few dreams, and not take life so seriously.

We offer many types of classes, including painting, in all mediums, wood-shop, landscape design, and yes, even a few writing classes. Mignonne has even gotten one of the local community colleges to accredit two of the *Writing 101* classes she teaches. She still writes, of course, and occasionally travels to give a lecture or two. During those times, I feel she has a pretty good substitute, not someone she would dare leave her class with for a long time, but someone she trusts to follow her curriculum...some of the time. The majority of the students seem to enjoy an occasional break from Mignonne's conservative, non-fiction criteria, and don't seem too offended by the more open minded, easy going writing style of their temporary professor.

At least, they act like they enjoy my part-time teaching.

I'm standing on the porch when Mignonne appears and calls for everyone to take their places. The crowd of people, which seems to be all of Franklin, is quick to obey, and takes position around the pond.

Ms. Mona and Clarence come out onto the porch and, as usual, Mona is picking Clarence. "Sugar, you still have your apron on under your suit coat. Just because you're catering doesn't mean you have to wear it the entire time."

"Sorry, Hon, just forgot, is all." He takes off his jacket, removes the apron, and tosses it back into the kitchen. "I think I look more natural wearin' it though."

"Get yourself down those steps and over to the pond," she orders with a swat to his behind. She then turns to me and Mignonne and I see that she's crying.

We come together in a group hug.

"Scott. Mignonne. What you've done is so wonderful."

We move apart and Mona takes my hand. "Scott, I think Jason would be so proud and happy with your decision."

"Thank you, Mona. I hope so. Now get down there with your husband before those young girls get him."

"Pshaw, no woman in her right mind would have him," she laughs. "Guess that's why we've been together so long." She heads off in a flutter of ruffles and big hair.

Lucinda is next out the door, breathtaking in a simple pink sundress that beautifully accents her olive skin and raven hair.

"Mignonne," she says excitedly. "I think we're about ready."

"Well then," Mignonne nods. "I guess I had better take *my* place at the flamingo cottage." She stands on her tip-toes and kisses me. "I love you."

"I love you too," I say as she passes Lucinda and heads down the steps. "With all of my heart."

She winks.

"I'm right behind you," Lucinda calls to her, then turns to me. "Because of you, Scott, I think this has turned out better than Jason ever imagined. Thank you for that."

I take her hand. "It wasn't just me, Lucinda. It was you and Clarence and Mona everyone that loved Jason Maler."

We hug; then I kiss her on the forehead. As she walks away, I look down and take in the incredible scene below. A large lattice and wisteria covered gazebo sits beside the pond, and surrounding it are at least two-hundred people who have come to celebrate with us today.

SQUAWK

The flamingoes have grown curious and are moving towards the gazebo as well, out of curiosity or perhaps as a sign of approval and acceptance, or...who knows...maybe they just want to be a part of the festivities.

You see...we're having a wedding here today. The couple who run the estate and oversee the school are getting married, and as part of their wedding gift, Mignonne and I have given them the farm to make their home. They are a wonderful couple, and we are so pleased to have them as part of our family.

A rather cold, gentle breeze wafts over me and I shiver. Odd, considering the temperature is in the high seventies, unless...

I look to the sky and smile. "Hey, Jason." His spirit seems to be with me, bringing with it a feeling of happiness and contentment. The breeze blows a bit harder and I get the point.

"Okay, you ghost. I'll go get him." I move to the open door and shout, "Hey, Buddy! You need to get moving or they're going to start without us."

Pat bursts though the door, still fiddling with his tie. "Calm down. It's not like they can start without me."

I straighten his tie and have a flashback of high school graduation. The three of us thought we were really something, standing there in front of the mirror, putting on our ties, caps, and gowns, believing *that* would be the biggest night of our lives.

Clarence begins playing his guitar, and like a songbird, Ms. Mona sings a pretty ballad while the guests take their seats.

Pat and I walk down the steps, march across the grass, and take our place in the gazebo with the minister. When Mona finishes her song, we see Lucinda waving, signaling that the bride is ready. The minister nods to Clarence, who clears his throat and who seems a bit nervous.

"I wrote this many years ago for my wonderful wife, Mona. And we decided that we wanted to give Pat and Sherry our love song."

He begins playing a beautiful, sweet melody that I don't recognize, but when he sings, the lyrics ring so true to the day.

We have wandered through our lives, a little sad and somewhat lost.
We've walked on separate paths, so many years at such a cost.
Finally those paths have joined, and hand in hand we'll go.
Throughout the wondrous journey...
Of our lives.

I nudge Pat. "Hey, the old coot's pretty good."

Pat nods but says nothing.

At that moment, Mignonne and Lucinda gracefully walk out from behind the flamingo cottage, the prettiest bridesmaids I have ever seen. When they are settled across from Pat and I, Clarence raises his voice a little, punctuating the chorus of the song that fits so well into this ceremony.

Our time has come today, when I will promise you my love.
Life is starting over, Heaven has blessed us from above.
My heart is overflowing and I know just what to do…
Get on my knees and pray…
And give thanks to dear God for…sending me…
Someone like you.

Sherry appears, and other than Mignonne, I don't think I have ever seen a more beautiful woman. She's wearing an ivory sundress, simple, yet elegant, and she's barefoot. Her auburn hair hangs in loose curls and in her hands she carries a small bouquet of sunflowers picked just moments ago. I glance at Pat and see that he's crying. My hearts soars, knowing that these two have finally found the love that has escaped them for so long.

I'm not crying…yet. Instead I'm smiling, as I realize that maybe…Jason knew what he was doing all along.

As the ceremony proceeds, my mind wanders, recalling this past year that has been so affected by the life *and* death of Jason Maler. I look at Mignonne standing there looking so beautiful, then glance over my shoulder in time to see Clay and Cameron subtly trying to keep the flamingoes away from the buffet.

The tears come as I realize how truly blessed I am. I have love, family, friendship, and…hopefully, a best seller.

In the past year, when I wasn't teaching Mignonne's class, I was writing. It's a short, simple, fact-based book, inspired by two incredibly memorable events in my life. My agent and publisher loved it, and so did the people in Hollywood. The movie rights have been sold and I have decided to give half of those proceeds to the Jason Maler Foundation because, honestly, if it weren't for Jason there wouldn't be a book.

It was my first attempt at non-fiction and will probably be my last because it requires tons of research and fact checking. It's harder to write the truth. Let's face it, that's Mignonne's field, and she was a great help.

However, I will admit this one came fairly easy. In fact, it seemed to almost write itself, not because I'm that talented, but because *I lived it...*

...Jason Maler's life and *The Summer of the Pink Flamingoes.*